I0831302

Malum in Se

Malum in Se

Five Tales

E.M. SCHORB

ISBN: 978-0-692-90525-8

Acknowledgements:

Grateful acknowledgement is given to the following publications in which some of these pieces first appeared:

Best American Fantasy, Gargoyle, Ginosko Literary Journal, OffCourse Literary Journal, Main Street Rag, The Mississippi Review, Mudfish, and *Poetry Salzburg Review.*

Cover portrait "Man in Hat" by E.M. Schorb.

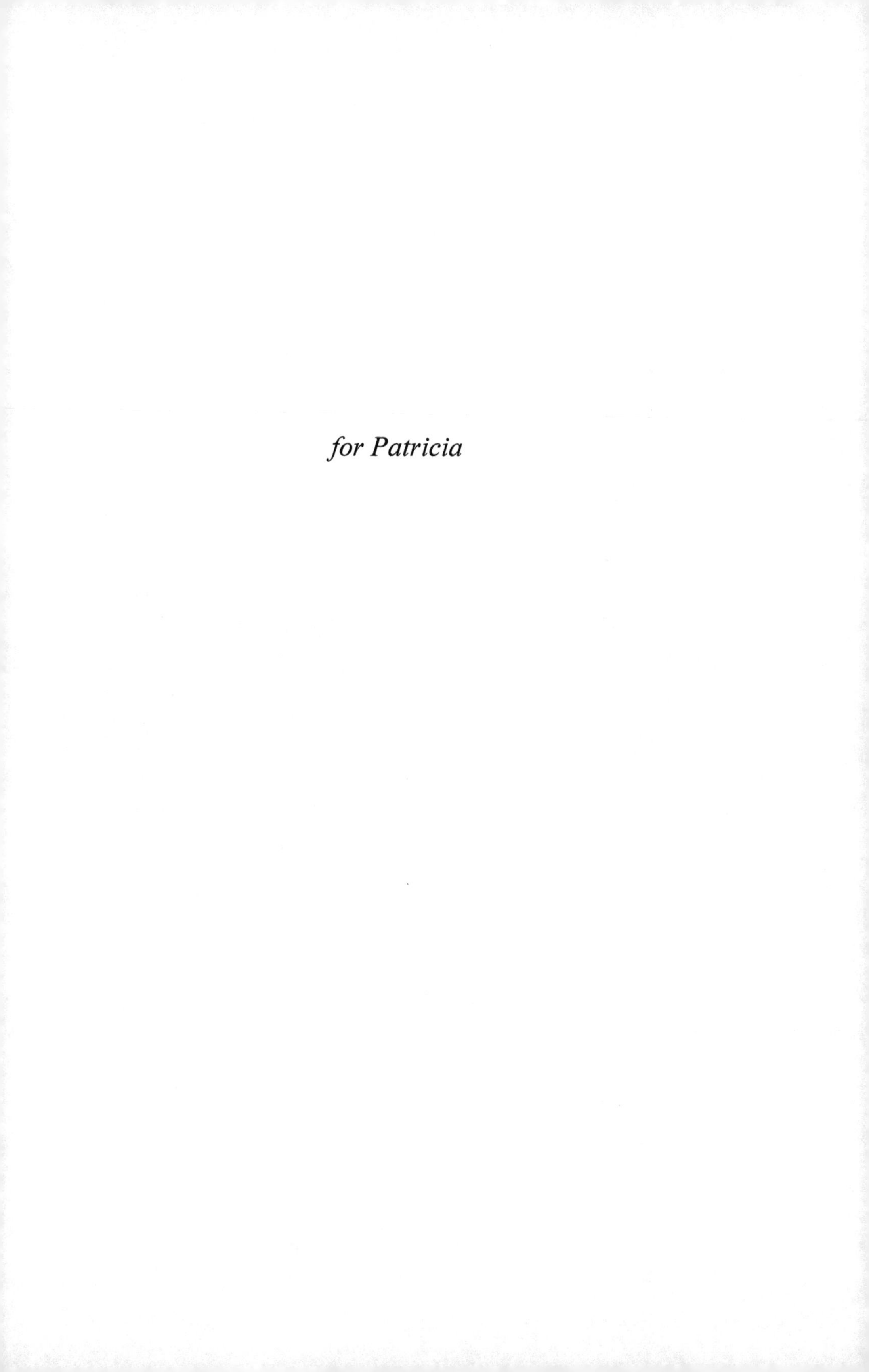

for Patricia

CONTENTS

Life is, in fact, a battle. Evil is insolent and strong; beauty enchanting, but rare; goodness very apt to be weak; folly very apt to be defiant; wickedness to carry the day; imbeciles to be in great places, people of sense in small, and mankind generally unhappy. But the world as it stands is no narrow illusion, no phantasm, no evil dream of the night; we wake up to it, forever and ever; and we can neither forget it nor deny it nor dispense with it.

—*Henry James*

Good can imagine Evil, but
Evil cannot imagine Good.

—*W.H. Auden*

PART I.

THE TERRIBLE SHADOW

Mind free of the terrible shadow of death, the child, who had gathered itself in the womb and could no longer remember its long genetic history, nor the gunmetal black un-time before it, sprang forth and grew until a time came when a whisper of futurity touched its quivering nerves; but still, mind free of the terrible shadow of death, felt by its mother and father, the child played in a place of organic magic, eating gummy worms and studying the dirt forming under its nails; now, mind free of the terrible shadow of death, the child attended the properly appointed and appropriate schools at each required stage, suffering often, but often joyful beyond adult reason—a bright kite flew, an airplane left a jet trail, a rainbow appeared out of the blue—and the shadow began to form, the terrible shadow of death. Mind no longer free of the terrible shadow of death, the child wrinkled like an overripe fruit, grew old, felt the terrible shadow of death, and died; then, no more mind, the child became the shadow.

LEGACY

He that hath wife and children
hath given hostages to fortune . . .
—Francis Bacon, Essays

I.

Biology, loneliness, and love have always been busy on Fortune Island; even now, no doubt, in the year 2000, when the island is almost completely deserted, when all that is left at least of the human aspect of things is the administrative building housing the few officials who tend to its history, natural and human. To the best of my knowledge, the island was named for a plundered and derelict Spanish galleon, the *Buena Fortuna*, that, according to one history, "scuttled on the treacherous Outer Banks of North Carolina" in the Sixteenth Century. It's said that the gathering dunes eventually buried all but the prow of the ship, leaving only half of the name in plain sight, and so newcomers to the island looked upon the name of the ship as the name of the island and Fortune Island it became.

By the Eighteenth Century Fortune Island was a considerable port-of-call, with a fluxuating population of around eight hundred people. These included fishers, shrimpers, lobstermen, and tradesmen of all sorts involved with water traffic, and, of course, in many cases, their families. But then the great disasters occurred, one upon another. A hurricane in the mid-Nineteenth Century shut the main inlet while opening another miles up the Banks. People left in droves for the new port. The "fixed" population dropped to about a hundred, and continued to drop with the coming of Union troops during the Civil War. When the troops withdrew at war's end, Fortune Island was virtually depopulated, a deserted island.

As you may remember, David, it is a whale-shaped island, its head to the north and out to sea, its finlike tail pointing southwest to the mainland. Most of the northern end, or head, is covered with enormous dunes, as if the sea view had been walled away. The roots of the dunes are entangled with the roots of mummified trees which once stood tall in the sea wind but now are buried and grip the depths of the dunes like anchors. The tail of the whale, the low narrow leeward end, was, in my time, where most of the population, a few fishermen and shrimpers mainly, had little houses along little streets of a village in miniature. A small white church with a steeple that one could see from the heights of Whalehead, near where my grandparents had constructed their own house, was the spiritual center of the island. Out behind it were two cemeteries, one for black folk, one for white, each with a white picket fence not meant to keep people out but apparently to keep our ancestral ghosts in.

I grew up on Fortune Island at a time when the outside world with its school authorities did not seek me out, there far across Pamlico Sound, as other truants on the mainland were sought. It was long before computers, remember. I was, to all intents and purposes, unknown to the mainland world of Beaufort, Moorehead City, and Wilmington, where once and once only the man I then believed to be my father, the Sad Traveller himself—presumably sad with the grief and guilt of the world on his hunched shoulders, but probably what we would call today a manic-depressive, or a bi-polar type—the Reverend Jason P. Cogburn, had taken me on his preaching circuit.

Garcie, the black midwife who had brought me into this world and who continued to watch over me, had taken the mail boat up to Ocracoke Island to be with her dying brother, and so couldn't keep an eye on me that day, and the Reverend Cogburn, whom I always just called the "Traveller," was most reluctantly compelled to take his six-year-old charge with him, where in one church he leaned over me and shouted, "Do you believe?"

How could I believe anything coming from his twisted lips and smoke-blackened crooked teeth? Skinny, in his tight black suit, with his hunched shoulders, he seemed like a hooded snake leaping into the air on its tail, and I shouted, "No!" *No, no, no*, I did not believe what he said, anything he might say, because I knew what no one else there knew, that he had none of the love in him which he preached about so readily, that he had terrified me since my mother's suicide in the sea, and then he slapped me, slapped me, slapped me with his long hard fingers until, crying and half screaming, I lied in his embarrassed, angry, sweating face, shouting, Yes, yes, *yes*, that I did believe, but I did not and could not ever believe whatever it was he wanted me to believe, had never believed, whatever it was, coming from him.

I looked for help, protection, among the congregation; but nobody interfered with the Traveller, for he was the authority on discipline. He set his believers an object lesson on how to deal with their own recalcitrant children, and most especially with a blasphemer, in this case a six-year-old who had dared to say no to belief. Shouts of approval pierced my ears. After all, I couldn't know that this was what they were paying for, what they would fill the collection box with their coins and even their bills for. I had become, before their eyes, an example of the reformed and, finally, apparently, forgiven. But I was never reformed and remain unforgiven and unforgiving till this day.

After the Traveller's sermon (a shouting match with the devil, or, more likely, a colloquy between the devil and himself) I learned that we had been at a church on the banks of the Cape Fear River. I waited outside and could see across to the big city of Wilmington and I remember seeing what a sympathetic church lady told me were Liberty Ships, hundreds of them, it seemed, a mothballed fleet, a long line of gray masts against lines of gray cypress trees, ghostly reminders of the recent war, and that is how I date this event. "No need to cry," the lady said, wiping my eyes with her lacy pink handkerchief. "Praise God, we have defeated the foe."

II.

Congratulations, Ruthie, on graduating from Smith, like your mother and your Aunt Jessie, and now that I'm the proud father of a college graduate and a young woman of great promise, of a daughter who will someday—a day, I hope, far in the future—upon my demise go through my papers—no doubt consigning most of them to the shredder—I want you to be able to make a wise decision about the disposition of your Aunt Jessie's unfinished memoir, excerpted above. She claimed that that part of the memoir represented the earliest memory of her childhood, other than running about on the dunes and getting her toes wet in the sea, so I put it first. I have stuck with what appears to be the correct chronology throughout. It is a personal document, more like an elaborated letter, written to me for the purpose of deepening my understanding of our background. Upon my death, it will pass to you, and you may do with it as you see fit—write a biography (you *are* an English major), or a novel, maybe, or throw it in the fire.

Since your mother's death, there remain on earth but two people this memoir can effect, for good or ill, and they are you and me, and when it passes to you, only you. But you're a woman now, and I feel that you should know what is contained in these pages. With your upbringing, some of it may prove shocking to your sensibilities, but I hope that I am not mistaken in believing that your humanity will manifest itself in understanding and compassion. Your aunt was a great woman. When I think of what she accomplished, against such odds, I am amazed. Of course, your grandmother, my mother after whom you are named, deserves much credit for what Jessie accomplished. But as you will see, your grandfather also deserves kudos for one of the most unselfish acts known to me. Alas, my dear, they are all dead and gone, and finally have nothing to fear.

I felt that the manuscript, incomplete, confused as a house of cards shaken to the table, needed a few words of interpretation and here I try to supply those words, so it is really a double memoir, one to me from Jessie, one from me to you. In love, faith, and trust, I am your father, David Perle, speaking to you from the present, which is, I hope, your distant past.

Jessie Judas, winner of the International Lamarck Prize in Science, the Kyoto Prize for Basic Sciences, and many other awards, died last month, at five o'clock in the morning of March 20, 2003, a cold rain battering the window next to her hospital bed near Chapel Hill, North Carolina.

A nurse told me that her last words were, "It's Hazel." In her delirium, the last throes of the cancer that had eaten much of her flesh away, she was about a half century off the mark, for Hurricane Hazel had struck, killing her beloved Garcie, in 1954, but what she said indicated her recent preoccupation with the past. In the deep subjectivity of the coma that came and went, and under the influence of many drugs, that past must have seemed like a dream, part fairy tale, part nightmare. And so at the end, she would laugh, frown, cry, and whimper, her dying mind still alive with it all.

She was cremated, according to her wishes, and her ashes were scattered from a high dune on Fortune Island to fly over sand, sea, and shoal, into Pamlico Sound west and into the Atlantic east in a maelstrom of salt air. A few of her former colleagues at the University and Duke, and even a couple who had come all the way down from the Woods Hole Oceanographic Institution, and one from the Scripps Institution in California—and I—attended. Adding to the general sadness of the occasion was the fact that you were unable to attend. (Ruthie, will you ever learn to stop taking chances? You are just like your grandmother Ruth—a daredevil. Please, for my sake, keep off those skis!) Of course Judas wasn't Jessie's real name; it was the name our father had assumed, apparently penitentially, a man who was too hard on himself, as I now see it. Tom Judas' real name was Thomas McQueen. Why Jessie had changed her name to Judas, I had not been able to understand until I read her memoir. It has been hard for me to decide what to think about this confessional piece, written, *in extremis*, when she had nothing to fear, least of all the truth. But I have added a few thoughts at the end of the manuscript with which you might agree.

About six months ago I heard that Jessie was ill, perhaps dying, and I broke off a sliver of time from my work at the State Department, work which had kept me at great distances from Jessie for many years, and went to visit her at her house in Chapel Hill. She was just sixty then—and at her death—and I found her radically changed from the tall, vibrant red-haired woman I had seen only a few years before. Then she had been the eminent scholar of a (to me) obscure branch of science, the author of several scholarly works and one book of personal essays on the academic life. But on this last visit I was shocked to find a frail, disheveled ghost of herself, her thick red hair become thin and ashen.

We spent a few hours together, reminiscing about our life together as kids in Boston. That was the only life I had known with Jessie, growing up at that Brookline estate my grandparents had built, and which was sold before you were born.

When I was a child, I assumed Jesse was my sister. Later my mother explained to me that she was my half-sister—though, at that time, I could not see any meaning in that minor distinction—still later, the mystery of Jesse Judas deepened for me because she didn't share our name. But what I chose to ignore or took for granted as a child, I felt compelled to ask about on this last visit, time being as short as Jessie's wispy, colorless hair.

"Why Judas?"

"I think our father took the name Judas," Jessie said, "out of guilt for a failure of character—and only once in his life did his character fail him, as far as I know, and for which he paid a high price, not in what others exacted from him for it, but in the price he exacted from himself—he assumed the name Judas, and I for much the same reason, I guess, decided to carry it on."

"Why? What did he do? What did you do? I wish I knew more about the past, Jessie."

"You will."

"But there's no one left but you to tell me."

"And I'll soon be gone. But you'll know all about it."

"How?"

"You'll see. And when you know the whole story, I hope you'll have . . . well, strength and forgiveness."

"Whom shall I need to forgive?"

"All of us—your mother, your father, and me—and me especially." She coughed, waved the subject away.

She looked both imperious and weak. I decided not to tax her with my insistence, and changed the subject.

"Do you remember the time we went to Fortune Island?"

"Do you? You were only about seven. By then there was no one there but the people from the National Park Service—a few public historical buildings—but Ruth and I knew where all the real people and places were. We went to the house where I was born, which really wasn't there, you understand, but was a ghost house, and we walked through it with all its good and evil memories"—she seemed not to be talking to me anymore but simply remembering out loud— "and we went to the cottage where Ruth once lived, and we walked through the rooms where she wrote one of her books and where she began to teach me and possibly where you were conceived. Mind you, nothing on the dunes but thin air."

"An insubstantial pageant faded."

"Yes. Ghosts. I hope to join them soon."

And too soon I had to be on my way, sorry to leave Jessie in such a condition and fairly certain that I would never see her again. Well, we had never seen much of each other. By the time I had entered high school she was already a graduate student. We were fond of each other, but she seemed always mysterious to me, a pleasantly bound but mostly closed book, and anyway more like an aunt than a half-sister, being fifteen or so years older. When I think about it now, Ruthie, I realize that I knew very little about her. But before leaving her on that last visit, she pushed a manuscript upon me, saying, "It's a piece of the story of my life. And yours. You might find it of interest."

And now I know why she and my mother always seemed in league against me when I showed them that I had a certain curiosity about aspects of the past, particularly about my father. Mother and Jessie would glance at each other conspiratorially and change the subject. Their unforthcoming behavior only served to make me more curious, but they were adamant, and I remained curious to no end. There was a secret between them, and I finally decided (for I loved and trusted them both, despite their odd behavior, because, after all, they lavished their love on me) that they would tell me the whole story in due time. I guess that's why I became a diplomat. My talent is patience.

III.

Dear David, over the years I've kept journals, diaries, scraps, and they've helped to keep my memory fresh. The following is for you:

I was born in a ramshackle house on Fortune Island, North Carolina in 1942 with the help of a black midwife named Garcie Cannon and very little else. That area of the Atlantic just off shore from the Banks was then known as "Torpedo Junction." German U-boats—submarines to the unhistorical modern—were sinking hundreds of merchant ships out there on that "stormy moat," as the poet Robinson Jeffers called it. I have been told that the fires of these sinking ships at night lighted the sky for miles. I have been told that I was born by that strange sinister firelight. Perhaps even as I was being born, our father's ship, just a few miles offshore, was torpedoed. He was about nineteen years old then, and had joined the Merchant Marines. Garcie told me that when he woke in the hospital in Raleigh, his hair had turned gray. This phenomenon of shock is called alopecia areata. It must have seemed strange to see such a thick head of gray hair on a man with such a youthful face. Our father, Tom McQueen, had inherited the house from his father and mother, a fisherman and a former schoolmarm, both dead before I could know them. How they came to live on that remote island I do not know, but I've always imagined that there must have been a great love story in it. Who else but lovers would suffer such a life, with no electricity, an outbuilding for cooking, so that the kerosene fumes wouldn't sicken them, and sand so deep and shifting that no car could maneuver it very far without getting stuck up to its running boards? Yes, David, in those days cars still had running boards.

As I say, I was born in that clapboard house with a production of Götterdämmerung going on outside at sea, where our father was being torpedoed into alopecia areata, or so I have come to think of the situation—which, in itself, sounds unpromising enough, but later Garcie elaborated it for me: "You were a long, skinny baby with a lot of red hair and I had to fight to get you untangled from your own cord. Your mamma wasn't strong, and a weakness in her chest caused her to cough and spit up blood." That was Garcie when I was ten or so. And from before that, the Traveller preaching over my mother, her on her knees before him: "You whored your way down from the mountains and across the Piedmont to the cities of sin on the coast—to Wilmington and the shipyards and the only man that would marry you, carrying his misbegotten child, that armed robber who's serving his sentence in Central Prison in Raleigh for trying to rob the payroll of the company that makes Liberty Ships to help fight our enemies. What do you say for yourself? Speak! Can't you speak? Never mind. You have nothing to say. Only pray, pray, pray," and I have an infant's image, whether real or imagined, of my poor mother, her pale skin flushed, coughing and spitting, and asking, begging, imploring, "When will you forgive me, when will you ever forgive me?" And him, drunk: "Never! Only God can forgive you!"

Do I remember this or have I made it up out of Garcie's palaver? I could only have been two or three years old. And one day my mother must have walked into the sea, because she was gone for several days, vanished, and finally her body washed up on the shore, her frail feet and curled toes tangled in green weeds, I have been told, her red hair in dark strands against her iron gray face, like a beached mermaid. Then I had only the Traveller and Garcie, only Garcie really, and she needed a lot of help from me by that time, because her eyes were failing fast, her diabetes winning against the light.

They took my mother's body to the hard sand near the shore, and there was trouble with the mail boat, causing a delay, so she waited for two days in the back of an old station wagon, waited to be taken somewhere for medical examination before being brought back to the island for burial. I went there to be near her and squatted next to the station wagon. I talked to her through the window. The owner of the station wagon came and opened the door and there was a terrible stench from inside and he threw some liquid into the back seat, for the smell, and shut and locked the doors. I waved goodbye when they took her body out in the skiff to the mail boat, even though I knew by then that she couldn't see that I was waving, or maybe I thought that she could see me from some other place. Because of the Traveller, I do not believe in other places any more.

Of course I knew by then that the Sad Traveller, the Reverend Jason Cogburn, wasn't my father—he had made that very clear to me—that my father was an evil criminal named McQueen who was in a prison everyone called "The Wall." I hated my real father as much as I hated the Traveller; sometimes more, because he had deserted me by committing a crime and going behind the Wall and leaving me with the Traveller for a father. I didn't know which one I hated most. I suppose I prayed to God to give me someone beside poor blind Garcie. Because of the Traveller, I don't think I believe in God anymore.

Jessie McQueen. I didn't want that last name. I was ashamed of it. And I was certainly determined never to call myself Cogburn, although the Traveller never asked me to. I was nobody. I belonged to nobody. I lived in the house where I was born, which now seemed to belong to the Traveller, and, when I was lucky, I was treated by him as a step-daughter, and, when not so lucky, he treated me as he had treated my mother. He drank heavily whenever he came home and I was afraid when he did and I would go over to Garcie's to stay with her, unless he demanded that I stay with him, which he sometimes did, when he had grown tired of talking to himself and felt the need of someone to torment.

One day I climbed the stairs to the small attic that was crowded with old damp boxes to see if I could find any of my mother's, or even of my grandmother's, clothes—the Traveller would occasionally bring me something back from his trips—but I was barefoot and in rags most of the time. It didn't make much difference on the island anyway, I guess; but I did need some things badly, and there among the boxes I discovered my father's books. The Traveller had taught me to read the Bible, and there was a dictionary among the books, and so I found a secret life for myself, a life away from the Traveller, away from the world. In the real world I was sinking deeper into my own isolation, but in the world of imagination, I began to expand. I called these books my secret treasure trove, and, handling them, touching them I could touch my father, who had smeared and dogeared almost every page. His mother, my grandmother, the schoolmarm, must have been my father's teacher, must have directed him in his reading. I could feel her hand on the books too. I put my fingers on her fingerprints. I could feel them in the attic with me, my father and even my grandmother. I could imagine him as a boy of my own age, curled up and reading *Tales from Shakespeare* by Charles Lamb, reading the *Essays* of Francis Bacon, especially the mystery of *The New Atlantis,* which was the mystery of an island like the one I was on. I discovered that Francis Bacon wrote that knowledge was power, and I, being powerless, took that to mean that my only way out of my life of subservience (though of course I didn't know such a word at that time) was through learning, and I set out to educate myself and have never hesitated in my quest for knowledge since.

It occurred to me that day up in the attic, thumbing through those books, that my father must have absorbed some of the things that I was reading helter-skelter and only partially understanding, like Bacon, that in his mind up there in Central Prison at Raleigh behind the Wall he must still possess chunks of Shakespeare, particles at least of Thomas Wolfe—because there was a dogeared copy of *Look Homeward, Angel* and another of *You Can't Go Home Again.* He had underlined passages, and I tried to glean what he had read and to put it into my own mind. There were books of poetry, mildewed but readable, books by Poe, Sidney Lanier, and Walt Whitman. There was one that I read as best I could, and re-read for several years—*Of The Imitation of Christ* by Thomas à Kempis. "To achieve this," my father had written in the flyleaf in a round young hand, "is to achieve perfection." Then how could he have done what he did? How could he have become a criminal? How could he have left me alone? How could he have left me at the mercy of the Traveller? "He that has wife and children hath given hostages to fortune." To Fortune Island!

I found *Under the Sea Wind*, by someone named Rachel Carson at the bottom of one box. A woman. I didn't know then that women wrote books. It was a very exciting discovery. I was going to read it right away. I carried it out to the dunes with me and discovered that it was all about the dunes, about the little animals that I watched, about the wind and sea. Biology. About my own biology. I went over to ask Garcie about my biology.

"How did my mother and father meet, Garcie?"

"They met in Wilmington, how men and women meet."

"How?"

"I told you, baby, your daddy was a soft-hearted boy and I guess he done seen a poor gal down on her luck and decided to help her out. Next thing they married and back here and she pregnant with you and he off for the Merchant Marines and he sunk and in the hospital and you born and he back here and off again to do that awful payroll robbery and in prison and the Traveller come tell your momma she need him and don't need your daddy and here we are, you sitting there eatin' grits and me talking up a storm. Now stop asking questions and let old blind Garcie get some shuteye, like I need to shut 'em for the dark, ha, ha."

"But why did my mother give up on my dad? Why did she divorce him?"

"She was a poor, sad, weak creature, more to be pitied, who couldn't do for herself much less anyone else. Without a man she was like a dog with nobody to walk her. She was sick most of her life, child, sick and ignorant and frightened and always needing a man to guide her, to give her direction and protection. Weren't her fault. God just make some of us like that so that the rest who is stronger have some way of using their strength. Some is needy, some is good, and some is greedy. That's the way it works. Your father was strong most of the time with moments of weakness in him—one big moment, you might say. A little of the devil would get into him once in a while, like it gets into you when you go into one of your conniption fits, but he weren't no bad person like you being told by that Traveller. When he got out of that hospital with his hair all gray he was onliest just a youngan hisself, and he got talked into doing something he shouldn't ought to done, thinking it was the only way he had to help you and your mother. He was always the most guilt-suffering boy you ever did see, and I can bet you anything that he is suffering right now."

"What's it like where he is, Garcie?"

"They calls it the Wall, and he behind it. It's a big dark tower, like one of those castles in that Frankenstein movie, but I don't suppose you ever saw that. Don't suppose you ever saw a movie in your life, did you, baby?"

"No ma'am. You know I ain't never been off this island long enough to see anything, 'cepting I remember those Liberty boats I told you about."

"And you never stop talking about them, do you?"

"No ma'am. What if I went to school, Garcie?"

"Just give Garcie another job in minding you. The Traveller is schooling you, according to his way, and nobody argues so far. He don't want you to know some things."

"What things?"

"Don't ask me, he just don't, and he does the payin' around here."

"What things am I not supposed to know? I already know things he doesn't know that I know."

"Like what, pray tell?"

"Like knowledge is power."

"That's a big mouthful for a little skinny blue egg just been cracked open. Go on, now; let me get my nap."

I went walking in the shoal at low tide and looking at the little whelklings in their tubes. I picked one from the clear water and held it in my palmed hands and I remember, I prayed to it: Please, give me someone. I dropped it back with a tiny splash and stopped, listening, waiting. No voice from the blue but the laughter of the black-capped gulls, laughter half drowned in the sea-smelling, soft, salt roar of the wind, and the susurrus of the shifting dunes.

Beaufort Inlet
Drum Inlet
Ocracoke Inlet
Hatteras Inlet
Oregon Inlet

—the ways in and the ways out. Why do they call them Inlets? They are Outlets. Like my mother, who came down from the mountains and across the Piedmont and finally out to sea—those waters, my mother.

If I had understood the word, I'd have known that the Traveller was a sadist. He made me cry whenever he could. "Look what I've brought back for you from Wilmington," he said one day after his return from his preaching circuit. His black coat hung on a hook inside the front door. He went to it and found something and tossed it on the table, across from his bottle of bourbon. A magazine: "True Crimes." I was about twelve. He sat leering at me as I tried to understand the meaning of the odd gift.

"Go ahead," he said, "look through it." I was sipping coffee. I put down my cup and thumbed through the magazine. "Find an article called 'The Case of the Disgraceful Vets,' he said. "There's a picture of your daddy there, and three others who were involved in that botched robbery." He put a square flat index finger on the page.

"That one—Tom McQueen—that's your father. How do you like him in his prison uniform? That's the man your mother loved. That man—not me. No matter what she said, she couldn't make me believe she loved me as she had that man. Damned and evildoers, both of them. And you had better watch yourself or you'll end up a wicked painted woman and a suicide, or like your daddy, a criminal behind bars. I'm watching you, but I can't always be here, so you better watch yourself. It's their blood that's in you. Where do you think you're going, young lady?" He tried, but he was too drunk to get up. "Hey, where do you think you're going?"

I took the magazine and grabbed my book and a blanket and went out on to the dunes on the sound side, found a comfortable place, and read about how my father and his friends had found the police waiting for them when they arrived at the shipyard. It seemed that the wife of one of the robbers had informed on them. The War was still on then and they were called disgraces to the uniform of the United States military and naval services and sentenced to ten years each. I studied the blurry photographs on the pulp paper of the magazine pages. All I could tell from the pictures was that they seemed young, except for my father who seemed old with his pale hair. But I knew that he was as young as the others. I remembered a photograph of him from the boxes in the attic. In that picture he must have been about my own age, twelve or thirteen, and his hair was raveny dark, the way I always thought of him. I understood that he was a criminal and in jail. But I couldn't believe he was really a bad man. I wondered how he'd forgotten what he'd read in *The Imitation of Christ.* Does it just slip away sometimes when you aren't looking? I lost my temper sometimes, so sudden it was scary. I'd yell mean things at Garcie. Once I even pushed her, and I was so sorry afterwards I cried and cried, and finally I cried myself to sleep.

When night comes to Fortune Island, it is like a big hand reaching out from the mainland, its fingers making dark shadows among the dunes, but for a time before that happens, there can be an horizonless silver of sound-water and sky until it darkens and to the northeast the soft steady recurring blink of the lighthouse appears in the dark like a star that you can almost reach out and touch, a star you can make a wish upon. I often empathized with the oyster, that, as it shuts its mother-of-pearl-lined shell, creates its own night, but its stars dim and die while ours spangle the sky.

More and more often, as I grew up, and the Traveller returned from his circuit, I would sleep out on the dunes and stare up, before, like the oyster's, the shell of my mind closed with my eyelids on the pictures they seemed to make. I had tried the attic for escape but I didn't like the feeling of being trapped up there. What if he were to climb up behind me? There was a little cave, not much bigger than a rabbit hole, which I had dug out, under the back wall of the house, and when it was raining or cold or both I would pile on my clothes and take my blanket and go there to sleep, but most of the time I would sleep with the other small creatures in the sand that walked with the wind. But some of the creatures on the dunes didn't sleep at night—the mosquitoes and sand fleas, "all those danged bloodsuckers," as Garcie called them—and I suppose it was a tiny crab that had crawled into my blanket that night that woke me, caused me to jump up and shake out the blanket. I heard a woman's voice behind me scream and then begin to laugh.

"Oh my God! You scared the bejesus out of me. I thought this place was deserted."

"Don't be scared. I'm just a little girl."

"Not so little, stretch."

"I'm tall for my age."

"Which is?"

"Twelve going on thirteen."

"What are you doing out here so late?"

"I was sleeping."

"Sleeping in the sand? Don't you have a bed at home? It must be three in the morning."

"I didn't want to be in the house with my stepfather. He's drunk."

"Oh you poor kid! Is he mean to you?"

"He's mean as a snake."

The woman frowned. "Does he hit you?"

"He tries, but I can dodge him most of the time."

"What does your mother say?"

"She's dead."

"Oh, I'm sorry to hear that. Well, don't you have somewhere you can go? A friend's house?"

"I can go to Garcie, but he looks for me there. I don't want to bring her any trouble."

"Garcie is your friend? An older woman?"

"She looks after me. She born me into the world."

"Not your mother—"

"Garcie's black. She's too old for any excitement. She was the midwife that helped to bring me in."

"I see. Well, my name is Ruth Perle." She gave me her hand to shake. It was warm and soft, but strong.

And that was the way Ruth always seemed to me: warm and soft and strong and firm and brave.

"I never heard anyone talk like you." I said. "You're not from around here, are you?"

"I'm from Boston. Up north. I'm doing some work down here—on the Banks."

"What work is there to do down here—if you're not a fisherman or a boat-builder or—" What else was there?

"Never mind about that now. Why don't you come on home with me and spend the night? Are you hungry? I can fix you something."

"That'd be mighty nice of you. I didn't eat any dinner or supper."

"Well, come on then." Ruth had not let go of my hand, and now she led me off across the dunes, stumbling and sliding and laughing—together! The words of our meeting may not be exact, blown away, as they were, by the night wind, but that was the gist of it. What I couldn't know then was that I had found my someone, the someone I had so long prayed to the sky and the sand and sea to find, prayed to the whelklings, the someone whose voice I had often heard murmuring inside the seashell, the friend from another world.

"Are you married?" I asked her.

"I was. My husband was killed in Korea."

"Mr. Perle?"

"No, no, I never used my husband's name. I was a writer when I met him and I'm a writer now."

"You mean like Rachel Carson? Look, I've got a book by her," and I waved *Under the Sea Wind* under Ruth's nose.

"No, not like Rachel Carson. I'm a folklorist."

"Oh," I said, vaguely disappointed, and wondering what that meant, but also still thrilled at the idea of meeting a real woman writer. "Do many women write books? I never heard of any before Rachel Carson."

"You never heard of Margaret Mitchell?"

"No ma'am."

"Who wrote *Gone With the Wind*?"

"No ma'am."

"Unbelievable!" Ruth exclaimed.

I was vaguely hurt. "I ain't never been off this island, excepting once when I saw the Liberty ships near Wilmington."

"Well, hell's bells, I found myself a Caspar Hauser."

"What's a Caspar Hauser?"

"A little boy who was kept away from the world."

"That's me, then—Caspar Hauser. But I'm Jessie McQueen—at least that's what they tell me, and they've been calling me that forever—well, as far back as I go."

I recognized the cottage we were heading toward. It had belonged, up until a few months before, to an elderly couple who had kept to themselves—almost hermits. There was a light inside, a golden glow at the window.

"What happened to the old people who lived here?"

"The wife died. The husband was taken off to a nursing home in Beaufort." She tugged and pushed at the door against drifted sand until she got it open. "Come on in—what did you say your name was again?"

"Jessie McQueen. The wife died and the husband is in a nursing home because he is so old," I said. "That's biology too."

Ruth looked at me as if I had said something very peculiar. "I suppose it is," she said, "in the larger sense."

"Oh, yes, ma'am, that's biology too. All animals die."

"I'm afraid I know that only too well, young lady."

"Yes, I suppose you do, ma'am. I didn't mean nothing by it. Just things come into my head sometimes and I out and say them."

Later, Ruth told me how I had startled her. She said, "I think I knew then and there that there was something very special about you." Every so often over the years she would remind me of what I had said that night and of its effect on her. "Come on in, Jessie McQueen," she said, in her hearty way, as I remember it, all those years back, those time-eaten years, and I couldn't know then that I was stepping through golden gates into my future, into a life I could never have imagined. As the deck has been dealt, approximately a year to a card, I look back on that moment as the first card dealt, an ace of hearts. I also look back on the vision before me in that little house, with each passing year, more and more, as a kind of Cinderella vision of the magic possible in a world I could not then have believed existed.

Ruth had the place lighted with several soft-gleaming oil lamps—remember, there was no electricity on Fortune Island then—that just kept awake the drowsy colors of hundreds of book jackets, and there were paintings—"prints," Ruth called them—on the walls done in styles that then were as alien to me as would have been a dinosaur or a spaceman; I had never seen anything like them. I had no idea, of course, but I was looking at prints of modern art: Van Gogh, Matisse, Picasso, Braque, all of whom and many more that I have come to consider familiar friends but who then seemed to me to be something from another universe.

"Oh, that's you!" I cried, seeing a black framed photograph dangling crookedly from a nail among the prints.

"That's me and my husband and my daughter. It was taken about ten years ago. Before you ask, my daughter is dead too. She died of polio when she was three. She would have been nearly your age by now."

"I'm sorry," I said meekly. I felt meek before such tragedy, but Ruth just smiled at me and shook her head. "That shouldn't be hanging there." She snatched the picture from its place and put it face down on a table. "People should be forward-looking. The future is our obstacle course with a pot of gold at the end."

Ruth was a tough-minded woman. If she hadn't been, David, she would never have been able to make the decision, on the spot, as it were, to surrender your father for my future's sake, as you will soon see that she did. But my eyes were still wandering in wonder. A Remington typewriter caught my interest, as a bright bauble catches the eye of a magpie. It was black and chrome and bulky with black keys with white letters on them. It seemed awesome, such efficiency, such power to make words on paper—and there was a half-typed page sticking out of it at the top. I couldn't take my eyes from it, now, even as I heard a cranking noise and music filled the room. I turned on my heel and there stood Ruth, smiling at me and tapping her foot to the music. "What is that?"

"I thought you could use a little cheering up," she said. "That's Glenn Miller, 'String of Pearls.' Well, what do you think of my humble abode?"

"If you mean this place—well, it's just wonderful! I've never seen anything like it. Our place is just bare boards, straight chairs, a table, and mattresses on the floor. The Traveller—that's what I call my step-father—he don't care about having anything around."

"Why do you call him the traveller?"

"He's a circuit preacher—on the road most of the time—which I'm glad for because I hate it when he's home. He comes home and drinks for a few days and goes off again and that's about all I see of him and I'm glad of it." I looked around. "Could you tell me what that is—that picture?"

"That's a Picasso print."

"What does print mean?"

"Well, it's not a real painting; it's a sort of photograph of the painting. And the painter's name is Picasso. The actual picture was painted way back in Nineteen-five."

"So long ago. . . But what is it? It looks like it's full of boxes."

"Do you like it?"

"I guess—sort of."

"That style of painting is called cubism. It does look like a pile of boxes, doesn't it?"

"All different colors—tan, yellow, and brown—but there's a fiddle sticking out of it—part of a fiddle, anyway. And there's a newspaper in some foreign language—what does that mean?"

"It's a French headline. It says—"

"But why is it like that?"

"Because Picasso thought it would be interesting to look at."

"It is—but, you know what? Your whole house is like that—what did you call it?"

"You mean cubism?"

"Uh-huh. All the books and everything—it's like cubism."

Ruth glanced about the room and laughed. "I suppose it is."

"I don't mean no insult. I just mean the books look like they're going to fall over—the stacks of them."

"I'm not the neatest person, young miss. Now how would you like something to eat? How about scrambled eggs and bacon? I'll go out back and rustle us up something. You go ahead and look around at anything that interest you. I won't be long."

The way we cooked on the Island then was in sheds back of the houses. We called them summer kitchens. We used them because the kerosene heat made the houses unbearably hot in summer. The stoves weren't good in those days and fumes could catch up with you, make you sick or even kill you. Ruth took a lamp and went out the back door. I was overwhelmed at seeing so many books in one place. I couldn't get over it. I would have said then that I'd gone dreamy. Oh, I couldn't believe what I was seeing; it was a book with Ruth's picture on the back—*Appalachian Tales*, by Ruth Perle. She did write books! And she was so beautiful too, with her huge almond eyes and her long dark hair, so smart and so beautiful and she was out back cooking me bacon and eggs. I had gone dreamy all right, no doubt about it. The smell of bacon came in first, then coffee, then Ruth with her fresh air smell. We were both hungry, eating fast and not talking much but a "Pass the salt, please," but Ruth finished first, wiping the last of the yolk from her plate with a last bit of bread. She lighted a cigarette—I hadn't seen a woman smoking before—and blew the smoke out with a contented sigh.

"Now tell me about yourself," she said. That's how I remember it—early morning, with the sky lightening outside, Ruth smoking and studying me with those big almond eyes—a word I learned later: chatoyant, her eyes—that looked like they could read your mind, and me, pent up with the story of my life on the verge of exploding from my lips, and a million questions waiting just behind it. Ruth let me ramble on for a long time before she finally stopped me with a question. She was lighting another cigarette and spoke around it.

"Are you really reading that Rachel Carson book?"

"Oh yes, I have a dictionary for the words I don't understand, though I can't find them all. But a lot of it is written like the Bible. You know, nice and simple. It's very beautiful."

"So you're interested in that sort of thing. I mean, the life of animals, sea life, biology?"

"It's funny: all my life I've lived right here and seen these little creatures running up the beach but I never really thought about them—they were just there. Then I found this book, and began reading about them, and, because of the pictures in the book, the drawings, I began to recognize them, and now I go looking for them. I want them to show me how they live. I've been pretty lonesome out here on this danged old island. No kids. No friends. Now it's like I have all these strange little friends. Fiddler crabs, and whelks, and the other day I met a huge ghost crab you could see right through—almost. I talked to him for about an hour. Then he went off about his business."

"What did he have to say?"

"That I'd be better off if I were invisible like him. But in a way I am almost invisible. No one knows I'm here."

"I can see you," Ruth said. "I know you're here. Come over here near the light and let me see your arms."

I stuck out my skinny, freckled arms for her to examine.

"Oh, you've been eaten alive," Ruth said. "I can't tell the freckles from the bites."

"The freckles are brown, the bites are red. I'm always like this except in the winter."

"You poor kid. I'll give you some citronella. Look at my arms." She held out shapely womanly arms with a tinge of dark hair on the forearms for me to observe. "I use citronella. It keeps the bugs away."

I was awestruck. This young woman from Boston knew more about living on Fortune Island than I did. I couldn't begin to imagine what else she might know, but I was to find out in the coming months.

"Miss Perle, I've been wondering, what were you doing out on the dunes so late at night?"

"My time is my own, sweetie—and call me Ruth. In fact, tomorrow I'm going up to Manteo."

"Where's that?"

"Right here on the Banks. Don't you know it? I'm going to see *The Lost Colony*."

"What's *The Lost Colony*?"

"A play by Paul Green—it's about Virginia Dare, the first English child born in America. Jessie, haven't you ever been off this island?"

"What I said, the Traveller took me on his circuit when Garcie was sick or busy or something and I remember seeing Wilmington—that's a very big city—from the other side of the Cape Fear River. I remember hundreds and hundreds of big ships."

"Listen, I have a wonderful idea. How would you like to go with me?"

I was so excited that it choked me. I nodded my head for fear that my voice would crack or come out in a squeal or a screech like an old owl.

"But you'll have to get your step-father's permission."

"Yes," I said, my pipes opening. "Oh yes!"

"Good. Now let's get a couple of hours sleep and then you can run home and ask if you can go. I'll open up that folding cot for you."

I lay in the dark but I couldn't sleep because I couldn't wait; but what if the Traveller wouldn't let me go? I would lie. That's all there was to it—I would lie my red head off. I would do anything to be able to go on this trip with Ruth Perle. I would not let anything stand in my way. I had to get off this island and see the world. *See the world!* The room was filled with light. Had I dreamed it all? No, it was true; for there was the astonishing Ruth, a reality, preparing for the trip.

In close to half a century, I don't think I've ever been so happy again as I was on that June morning in 1954, not even many years later when I received notice that I was awarded the Lamarck Prize. The joy I felt was like another being inside me trying to burst through my skin. I remember vividly the kinetic sense that my arms moved too fast, my skinny legs seemed to dance to the table for coffee, my head swiveled, not turned, but swiveled, and my heart pounded like a little drum in my chest. I ran across the hot sand of the dunes and for the first time in my life did not notice the heat. I might as well have been a skater on ice, I went so fast, the inner reaches of my mind my only hoveringly physical part, my dream come true. And there was no mean amount of fear. Why should I believe, hope, what would lead me to believe or hope that the Traveller would let me go? But I would lie. I would change my story and lie. I burst into the house and found that my worst fears were unwarranted. The Traveller was gone, off on his circuit once again. There was an envelope on the table—FOR GARCIE. Her money. I grabbed it and ran all the way to Garcie's shack. She had me count the money and read her the note. *Gone for about a week. Enough to keep her fed.*

"Later you take me to Walkup's to get some groceries, hear?" said Garcie.

"I'm going fishing, be back later."

"You watch yourself, now, child, hear?"

When I got back to Ruth's she had a tin tub filled with steaming water. She was naked but for a towel around her hair. I had never seen a woman completely naked before. Biology again! I lurched toward embarrassment but Ruth's matter-of-factness caught me back.

“Strip and get in there,” she said, and I followed her orders unquestioningly but full of questions.

“Well,” she said when I had stripped, “you’re not even a tabula rasa, you’re a bas relief of bites, abrasions, and bruises. Let me look in your mouth,” and she poked a forefinger around inside my gaping mouth with an intermittent hum as if she were looking for pearls and finding sand; but no, she pulled her finger from my mouth and said, “It’s amazing. Your teeth are in pretty good condition. I don’t suppose you get much candy, sweets, do you?”

“I don’t eat much of anything most of the time.”

Ruth said, “I’m going to take a picture of you, so we can check on your progress.” And she stood before me with the camera up to her face and the dark V of hair at the bottom of her belly, her breasts crushed together by her arms as she looked for range—and of course I have often seen what she was seeing that morning (I still have that treasured, faded photograph): a gawky, gangly stringbean of a girl topped with a mass of dark reddish hair that looked as though it had never come in contact with a comb. “Pop!” went the flashbulb and, momentarily blinded, I must have jumped a foot off the ground. Ruth, laughed, put down the camera and picked up a lighted cigarette, stuck it between her teeth—and I was laughing now—and said, “Into the water with you, young lady. I hope you don’t mind bathing in the same water that I just got out of, but we don’t have time for another tubful. Now I’m going to wash your hair and then I’m going to find you something to wear. I’ve got a pair of bluejeans that should fit you. We’ll have to roll the cuffs down, but otherwise . . .”

When we were dressed, Ruth took another photograph of me. In that picture, my hair is combed, and I'm wearing a sweatshirt with cut-off sleeves that has SMITH COLLEGE written across the front—the shirt is red and the lettering is gold—the jeans, a pair of Ruth's sandals, just a bit short, for my toes curl over the soles, and I'm proudly holding my first pocketbook, a small brown leather purse with a long thin strap to put over my shoulder. The strange thing is, I was twelve and except for my height I look younger in the first picture; in the second, I look like a young lady. It was the first time it had ever occurred to me that I might be—well, if not pretty, at least presentable in the way that young women ought to be, or ought to have been in the Fifties.

"Now here's our itinerary," said Ruth. I must have looked blank. "This is what we're going to do." And she told me as we trudged across the sand dunes with her logistical haversacks on our backs and cameras dangling from our shoulders. Ruth had explained that she had a tape recorder in a trunk in her "vehicle," which meant car, I guessed. We were heading to Sheriff Walkup's General Store, and working up quite a sweat getting there.

Walkup's General Store was the only store on Fortune Island, and was a good hike from Ruth's place. Walkup was a retired county sheriff then somewhere in his late sixties or early seventies, who had come to the island about twenty years before and opened the General Store, a two-story building the lower floor of which was the store and the upper floor the living quarters. He sold bait and tackle, canned goods, cereal grains, quite a variety of oddments, and was also the Postmaster. His wife was the wooden Indian figure at the cash register. On several occasions I had tried to make friends with her, but she had no interest in children. The most she ever showed me was cold tolerance.

We had to take Sheriff Walkup's skiff out to the mail boat, a pretty white little steamer about fifty feet long with green trim and a red, white, and black smoke-stack emitting dark, immediately dissipating little puffs against blue sky and white cloud, and followed by a great wing of happily screeching gulls. We climbed into the skiff and Sheriff Walkup began pulling at the oars, puff-ing and pulling, then stopped about thirty feet from the steamer to wipe his wet forehead with a damp handker-chief.

"I'm getting too old for this," he said; then, bright-ening, "Lookee yonder, ladies! You see that there feller waiting to get off? That's my new strong back standing there. Don't look like it, does he, in that there seersucker suit and straw Stetson, but I'm gonna have him in dirty work clothes before this skiff has to go out again," and he began painfully pulling at the oars once more while Ruth and I got a closer and closer look at the man on the steamer's deck.

"Look," I said, "he's got a guitar looks like."

"Good God," Ruth said, "he looks good enough to eat."

"He's beautiful," I whispered.

"Watch out, ladies," said Walkup. "He's mine."

We climbed a rope ladder and got aboard the mail boat as the stranger tipped his Stetson in greeting, helped us up with our paraphernalia, and handed down the mail bag, his guitar case, and a battered old suitcase to

Walkup. Up close, he looked just as good but surprisingly pale, as if maybe he had spent too much time in juke joints playing that old guitar. We hated to see him climb down into the skiff and row off with Sheriff Walkup. I wished he could come on our trip with us. All duded up like he was, it'd been fun to show him off, like something you'd won at a shooting gallery.

Everyone on board took this adventure for granted, or appeared to, but I thrilled at everything I could touch, smell, or see—the rust on the iron rails, the wake coming from the bow and scudding outward in white foam, the spindrift that dampened my hair, the sudden distance between us and Fortune Island, my home, that seemed so much less important to me now than the invisible place where we were to land, the wild gulls flying in our wake, and the wilder clouds racing across the blue sky. I had probably never felt so alive in all my long captivity. The lighthouse I often saw from Fortune Island, the one that seemed a low, twinkling star to me when I was younger, that always seemed disembodied, was soon looming before me, tall, conical and stark white. But before that, I looked back and saw a Stetson wave goodbye.

On Ocracoke, we squeezed into a pickup truck and were driven to the village, where Ruth unveiled yet another miracle. Behind a building, I think it was a restaurant, Ruth removed a tarpaulin with a "Voila!" to display an old Army jeep. I had never seen one before in my life. It was—exotic! It was dirty and rusty and tough looking as a flat-faced dog, and Ruth had it barking in no time—and bouncing, and bouncing—for I soon discovered that jeeps could go anywhere but they could not go anywhere without bouncing, and I had to hold on for dear life for fear of being tossed ten feet in the air and left on a beach somewhere, forgotten by Ruth, who seemed intent on nothing else but mastering this wild machine. We bounced, jumped, leaped on for fifteen miles, sometimes on the beach, sometimes on the road, sometimes, it seemed, we stayed in the air for miles on end. My first lovely hairdo was in wild disarray by the time we reached the Frazier Peele ferry landing at Hatteras Inlet, where they told us we had to drive our jeep up the planks and on to the ferry first because it was too heavy to lift—the ferry only held three cars: two were put side by side, then the men would lift the third so it would be behind the other two, crosswise. As we made the crossing to Hatteras, Ruth, apparently unfazed, spent some time re-shaping my hair. "I don't want you looking feral," she said. Again she could see I was blank.

"Like a wild girl," she said.

"Do I look like a wild girl, Ruth?"

"Not now," she said, smoothing back my hair, pushing here and there. "Now you look like you're ready for Atlantic City."

I pretended to know what she meant, but I couldn't help wondering if we were going to Atlantic City, too, wherever that was.

And then we were bouncing along again and Ruth didn't even slow down when we came to the Cape Hatteras lighthouse, which I was to learn was one of the most famous in the world. "That's the Cape Hatteras lighthouse," she called, dangerously taking her right hand from the jumping steering wheel of the jeep to point at what I thought was one of the greatest wonders that I had ever seen—in fact was one of the greatest wonders that I had ever seen, or almost seen, it receded so fast from view, like a lonely giant peppermint stick. I had to turn my head almost all the way around to face front. Everything was like that with Ruth—whizzbang!

"We're heading up Hatteras to Oregon Inlet," she yelled. I must have agreed. I had noticed by now that disagreeing with Ruth was useless. "Yes," I suppose I said, but then I yelled, "when are we going to stop to eat?"

"When we get there," Ruth yelled back over the growls of the jeep and the roar of the surf.

"Get where?" I yelled.

"Nag's Head," she yelled back. "I have friends there."

It hadn't occurred to me before that Ruth had friends on the Banks—I thought of her as all alone and from far away Boston. The realization that she had friends nearby raised another question in my mind. "But if you have friends, Ruth, why do you live so far away from them? Why do you live on Fortune Island, where there isn't hardly anybody but me and Garcie and just a few others?"

"Because it's the perfect place to write, my Honeylamb. I do my collecting up and down the Banks—like this—and then I bring it back to Fortune Island where there isn't anybody to bother me and I can concentrate and write."

I thought about that for a moment and then I said, "Ruth, am I going to bother you?"

She gave me a quick, disturbed look. "Not you, Honey, never you. Don't you ever worry about that." Then she gave me the warmest smile—at the same time maneuvering on the beach without looking forward. Ruth could do it all.

We crossed Oregon Inlet on a much bigger ferry. In fewer than twenty miles of paved road we came to a populated area. What chance of the flarings and dimmings of the lights of memory brings us back the past and what chance encloses it in darkness forever, I do not know. It seems to me now that we pulled into a big yard in front of a big, gabled house; it seems to me now that the yard was full of children, some younger than I and some older, boys and girls, young men and young women, and that the king and queen of the place, told by graying hair and other signs of advancing age, were in front of the children, or at the middle of the group, or did they appear at the sides of the jeep to help us out? I remember the steamer trunk in the back seat of the jeep being opened and a tape recorder being taken into the house. Greetings, lunch, and hours of taping the voice of our host, as I remember a burly man who told many strange stories of the folklore of the Banks, stories of storms and pirates, and Blackbeard. I especially remember songs, stories and songs all afternoon, Ruth changing reels of tape, taking notes, urging the man on to talk and sing more: and I remember my embarrassment at having to eat with the other children, which was the embarrassment of a stranger who had been isolated for so long at having to socialize with an advanced race of people her own age, fully civilized, knowledgeable young people, whose education had not been neglected to the point of mental infirmity as my own had been. No one actually said, "Are you a dunce?" but I heard it over and over in my mind and I thought I saw it in the eyes around me, but probably not, for everyone was extremely kind, I remember, and one girl who appeared to be about my own age helped me with a personal matter, a biological matter, that had just begun to be a serious consideration in my life.

Then Ruth and I left their house to go to the play, which was long and involved Sir Walter Raleigh, Queen Elizabeth, Indians, and the first English baby born in the new world, Virginia Dare. The image that time has left me is the image of the top of the ship's sail, a rough rectangle of white against the actual night sky, moving away behind the tops of the wooden stakes of the fort, sailing away and to England to get supplies and leaving the remaining colonists on their own—and of course they waited for the ship to return but it never did to their knowledge and they wandered into the woods and were never seen again. I broke down at that image of the sail against the night sky and Ruth took me in her arms and comforted me. I was tired. Emotionally exhausted. So when Ruth asked me If I would prefer to drive back home that night or to go back and stay with that nameless family, I told her that I wanted to go home. I wasn't used to people and the strain of making small talk, and smiling and trying to grasp what was expected of me was too much. I wanted to be alone with Ruth, racing with the moon at the edge of the sea. I fell asleep—even in that bucking bronco of a jeep.

And here I go blank. I only remember that the next morning, or was it the morning after, I woke and found myself back in Ruth's cottage, stretching my skinny self awake on her folding cot, smelling coffee. I lay there and thought about that sail, that tiptop of the sail, bellying the ship away, and the poor people who were left behind and lost forever. I could understand them. When the doctors recently informed me of my condition—terminal—the image of that sail flashed back as if I were there again, watching the play, and wanting to snuggle into Ruth's warm arms, Ruth. Ruth—my friend, my mentor, my mother, my sister, my benefactor, my everything but one.

"I told"—and Ruth named the patriarch of the family we had visited— "that you were interested in biology, and he gave me a copy of *The Science of Life,* by H.G. Wells. She held up a thick tome. "I ought to know more about biology myself, so do you know what we are going to do? We are going to read this book together, and anything you don't understand I will try to explain. If I can't, I'll get us some help." It took us something like two months to get through that book, with its enormous divisions of geological time making me feel smaller and smaller, like Tiny Alice, finally like an invisible dot, a fractal, and yet, as Ruth made me see, somehow, potentially anyway, more than I had imagined I could be. I began to see the life around me now as moving toward, if not perfection, adaptation, which, I saw, was a kind of temporary perfection, as near as dynamic Mother Nature lets us get to perfection. For things either get better or worse, depending on how you look at them, of course, what vantage point you take, but there is no stasis, no stopping of change; and of course things are ever so maladjusted, because forever trying to adapt themselves to ever-changing circumstances—yes, I saw that too. Not unlike myself. I saw myself as a little unimportant thing trying to adapt myself to my circumstances. I had not seen myself this way before. Before—what had I seen or understood? Nothing, or a blue blank. I had been a container of emotions carried about by the sea wind. I began to sense purpose. If not God's, my own. And my purpose should be partly of my choosing. I came to see that, or I was drawn out to see it, I suppose, by Ruth.

When the Traveller was away, Ruth took me on "field trips." Once we went to Wilmington, where Ruth bought me some clothes at Efird's Department Store, the fanciest store in town. I asked her to take me to the docks to see the Liberty Ships and was heartbroken to see that they were gone. How could I know now that I had ever seen them as my memory told me I had, hundreds of them in a row, and the gray cypresses behind them? Once we went to see the wild ponies on Shackleford Island. They are both of biological and folklorish interest. Once Ruth hired a motor launch to take us to Beaufort, a town not so big as Wilmington but much more beautiful, truly Old South, as Ruth might have said. There they gave a party for Ruth, the famous folklorist, "who has done so much to make the beauty and virtues of the Old North State known to the world through its voice in song and story," as the Mayor said in a speech that seemed to go on for hours. Now I realized that Ruth was not a stranger anywhere she went, but was widely known, unlike my unimportant self, of whom no one seemed aware. This realization didn't spur jealousy—I could never have been jealous of Ruth—but perhaps the first faint glimmers of ambition, the desire to do something important in the world, as Ruth had done: like her, but myself.

I had to introduce Ruth to Garcie. I had seen enough of Ruth in action to know that she would like and appreciate Garcie, and I was sure that Garcie would find Ruth an interesting subject of contemplation. They hit it right off. Garcie told Ruth some wonderful tales for her book.

A point of continuing interest between them was the Sad Traveller himself. I, in my "angel infancy," as Ruth called it, had not realized that Garcie did not like the Traveller. "I takes his money, yes I do, but I would always watch over my little Jessie even without his money. He a religious man? Maybe some, but in a crazy sort of way, too full of hate for me who believe in a loving God."

"Has he ever," Ruth said, turning to me, "has he ever—mistreated you?"

"You mean slapped me around?"

"Well—yes—but—anything else, either?"

"Sometimes. The last time he was home—he was drunk, he always gets drunk when he comes home; he says he needs to relax—I was wearing shorts and he walked behind me and touched me on my backside, but then he acted like it was an accident. I jumped away, and I was burning with shame—"

"And shock."

"Shock—yes, ma'am."

"Has he done that before?"

"No, that was the first time he ever did that, but he's slapped me around a lot of times."

Ruth looked worried. Garcie said, "These things happen to young girls. Can't say how many uncles I had growing up would pat my fanny."

"But it's not right," Ruth said.

"Lots of things not right, young lady."

Ruth conceded the point with a nod. But I could see that she was thinking of doing something and I was sorry that I had spoken out. I didn't want Ruth and the Traveller to get into a fight over me. I was afraid he might stop me from seeing her. I had tried to play down my friendship with Ruth. Garcie said you always come to a fork in the road of life, and then another and another, and on till the end. I didn't want to come to the next fork in the road of my life—I loved where I was, despite the Traveller and anything else that might spoil a moment of it here and now. Ruth told us about a folk singer and guitarist who met the devil at the crossroads and became great and died young. She said he had traded most of his life for a moment of glory, and that that was a mistake. I didn't know what to think about that, but it did make me think, and I guess that was the point. Ruth told us how she became a folklorist. She told us that growing up during the Depression had probably led her into Folklore. She was born in Twenty-nine and, thanks to her older brothers, had heard songs by Woody Guthrie and Leadbelly and others who could be described as folksingers from her earliest days, and, upon entering college, had started as an English major, but, with an ever-increasing interest in folklore, had decided to change over to anthropology, and, eventually, to the relatively new field of social anthropology—which amounted to becoming a folklorist.

"You mean you had to do all that anthro-business just to listen to people?" Garcie shook her head in consternation. "Well I must be one those anthro-people myself, cuz I have been listening to folks all my days. Finds, in fact, it's hard to get a word in edgewise, most folks telling about themselves until it's running out of my ears. Goodness sake!"

Ruth burst into laughter and couldn't stop until I thought she was going to have a heart attack. But finally she pulled herself together and said, "I'd love to have you make a speech to the anthropology department at Smith, Garcie, it would sure give them a shock." This time Garcie laughed.

By October, Ruth and Garcie and I had become a cozy threesome. We spent hours on end at Garcie's shack, cooking and eating together and Ruth and I listening to Garcie's legends of the Banks, of which she had an endless supply. Garcie did not like to be recorded, but Ruth kept her tales for posterity by making notes on yellow pads. Ruth later told me that listening to Garcie reminded her of blind Homer, and how the Greeks must have sat around the bards, for Ruth said that there were many Homers, and listened to their tales to the accompaniment of plinking lyres. "Garcie may be nearly blind," I said to Ruth, "but you're the Homer."

Ruth winked at me and said, "O.K., smarty pants, you got me there."

Garcie knew the inside of her small shack as a clam knows its shell. She knew her life and rolled breathlessly about in it without hesitation, telling one tale after another. She opened up to Ruth as she had never done with me, and so I heard much that I had never heard before. Ruth had a way of prompting people to talk, a subtle way of making them want to tell her things, and she was a good listener, as I had had occasion to observe, focusing her full attention on a speaker, letting him or her know with a word or two that she understood the import of what was being said. Her patience with a speaker was inexhaustible. Her eyes never drifted. It was an art, she said, that she had learned from acting in amateur productions when she was in college. "Don't be an actor, be a reactor," she often said.

I didn't know whether I wanted to be Ruth or just to have her to love. And Garcie could tell that I had found someone who almost replaced what I'd lost in a mother.

"You just crazy about that young woman, ain't you, baby? Well, she mighty nice indeed—mighty nice."

So we had a three-month interlude of pure happiness, or at least I did. But we were flying toward Garcie's fork in the road, or, more properly, it was flying toward us, like a great big black seventy-eight record with an album of booming cacophonous music on it. At its center it was turning at a hundred and fifty miles an hour, like a tornado, and coming at us at fifty at the rim. We had weathered storms before—twice only recently—but nothing like this, nothing like Hazel.

Late in the evening of Thursday, October 14th, 1954, Sheriff Walkup pounded on Garcie's door. "Bad storm coming," he said, stepping just inside, his yellow slicker glistening. "Better get prepared." His general store was powered by a generator, and he had a radio, which made him the unofficial town crier.

"Maybe you all should think about going to the mainland. There's a cutter down by the village picking up now. It'll be there for a few hours. Tom—that's my new man—he can take you out to it. It's up to you."

"We'll ride it out," Garcie said, "like we rode the last two out. But thank you for thinking about us."

"I hope you know what you're doing, Miss Perle," he said.

"We'll be fine," said Ruth, undaunted.

"Step out here and look at those clouds," said Walkup.

"You know I'm blind," said Garcie, but Ruth and I stepped out into a light, windy rain to look. Where had they come from, those dark, iridescent clouds, like malignant brains? They hadn't been there a few hours before, when we arrived at Garcie's.

"It'll be a good night for storytelling," said Ruth. Walkup shrugged and climbed back over the dunes like a goldfish out of water. He knew that the madly-rolling eye of the storm was looking at us, but he had given fair warning. I caught his voice—perhaps words of farewell—on the wind as he disappeared over the top of a dune.

Garcie said, "Ain't nothing but just another storm."

You must remember, David, things were very different a half century ago. Beach cottages didn't have radios, television sets, and newspapers were scarce—no front pages inked in red, green, and white hurricane winds swirling around a blank blue eye—so we sat on talking through Thursday night even as we could hear the wind about us dodging and ramming, missing and hitting, sputtering, cracking, and shockingly booming. We naively thought of it as good atmospherics for Garcie's tales of sunken ships and the ghosts of skull-and-crossbone pirates. Then she told us about the sunken church, inspired by the wind, I guess. It was cursed because its congregation was evil, and it would rise out at sea during evil times, as when a hurricane was on the way, and *that,* said Garcie, was the sound of banshee singing that forecast the storm. "At first," she said, "the storm is outside of you, and then you are inside of it, like old Jonah in the belly of the whale. But we've ridden out a few of them storms before and we do it again, my bet."

It was too noisy for us to sleep, so we sat on until dawn. Then a window broke and water gushed in. When the first wave receded, Ruth and I looked out and saw that everything from Whalehead down was under black or foaming white water, whirling, swirling all sorts of objects in its wake, then the windows shattered and the front door fell in and the debris laden tide filled the room. Except for one shriek, Garcie sat like stone in prayer, water already up to her hips, her body pummeled by broken objects. Ruth and I waded to the door and tried to stand it up, a hopeless task. Then Ruth grabbed me by the shoulder and pointed.

"Oh my God!" she cried. A shrimp boat, about forty feet long, was coming straight at us. The great dark hulk had been beached down by the village for repairs and had been lifted by the tide and now was drifting, without a mind to guide it, toward Whalehead. It was coming right at us when something, a twist of the wind, or a roof beam, something out there in the half-light, caught it and spun it like a top. Then it set off in another direction, its whole huge dark side passing in front of us like a wall that we ourselves were passing, but not quite passing: its bulk slammed into a corner of Garcie's shack and we found ourselves outside, the three of us, boards from the shack spinning around us, careening into us like little battering rams; and now we were up to our chests in whirling water, a maelstrom, and Ruth trying her best to keep Garcie from drowning. She swam and knocked away debris with one hand and pulled Garcie with the other, all the time screaming to me, "Are you all right? Are you all right?"

I went under and came up with a mouth full of salt water. I couldn't answer. I kept drifting away from the sound of her voice. Then I went under for what I thought was good, but a hand pulled me up by my hair and suddenly I was being pulled aboard a bouncing, bucking skiff. The hand laid me in the bottom like a caught fish, face down and vomiting brackish water. When I could look up, I saw Garcie's legs and Ruth's. I tried to get up on a cross bench and was nearly thrown out again, but pulled again by the hand and pressed down until I was sitting in the bottom of the skiff, my back against a man, his knees locking me in place. I had to see who he was and twisted my head to catch a glimpse of my savior—a glimpse of dark hair and pale face and I knew who it was.

Ahead, the dark and chopping Atlantic had seized everything but the second story of the General Store. We were headed for it. It was a good thing Sheriff Walkup wasn't pulling at the oars or we would never have made it, but, as Walkup had said, the new man had a new strong back. He was also a good sailor, for he found back-tows in the whirling water that helped him get us to the store. We climbed through a second story window and I fell to the floor.

I fell asleep and must have slept for several hours. I woke to dismal daylight and rain drumming on the tin roof. Mrs. Walkup, Ruth, and the new man were there, drinking coffee. Where was Garcie? "*Garcie*!" I screamed. "Where is Garcie?" They looked at me, then at Garcie. She lay over in a corner on the floor. "Garcie!" I threw myself on her, shaking her bulk, pulling at the rags that had been her dress. "Garcie, please! Wake up, please! Don't leave me, Garcie—please!"

"Her heart failed," said Ruth, lifting me away and holding me. "I'm so sorry, baby."

I looked around blankly, incomprehendingly. I stared out the window where we had come in. "Where's the water?" I said, as though distracting myself from "where's Garcie?".

"It was a storm surge," Ruth said. "It's all gone back to the sea."

"It was a hellion named Hazel," Mrs. Walkup said. Then she shook her head, "And she stole my husband, little darling" she said to me, and she seemed as uncomprehending as I was, or she never would have called me that. I felt so sorry for her that I took her in my arms and, for a moment, we seemed to do a slow dance together. I wanted to cry for her, and I wanted to cry for Garcie, but I couldn't, I felt like my spirit had left me and all I could do was to wait for it to return. And that was it—the others were in varying degrees in the same condition. I could see that now as my own shock subsided.

Ruth handed me a cup of hot coffee and told me to go over and thank the new man, Tom Judas, for saving my life. "He saved all of us, except for poor Garcie," she said. "He came out in that little skiff just to find us and bring us to safety." I looked at him. What an odd name, I thought. Judas betrayed Christ. It must be awful to have a name like that. I went over to him and said, "Thank you for saving my life, thank you for saving Ruth, and thank you for trying to save Garcie. It was wonderful what you did."

"The surge brought me right to your door," he said. He was sitting on the floor, still drenched. He didn't look the same. Of course he was exhausted, but what I mean is, that when we first saw him on the mail boat, he looked like he didn't belong; but now he was in work clothes and wet and disheveled as the rest of us and seemed to belong with us, seemed to belong to Fortune Island.

"You're a hero," I said. "Ruth, isn't Mr. Judas a hero?"

"More than a hero, I'd say. A savior."

"Yes—Mr. Judas, you're a savior."

His face, not so pale as it had been when I first saw him, showed a pink tinge of embarrassment, as if, for a second, he'd grown younger, almost boyish. "I was just trying to help," he said, the color fading as fast as it had come, the soberness reasserting itself. "I'm very sorry about your friend. You must have loved her very much."

"Yes, I did. I didn't know how much till now." I looked over at poor Garcie. She looked like a big wet pile of laundry—my Garcie—but Ruth was making her vanish beneath a blanket. "You get used to people, sometimes, Mr. Judas, and you forget how much they mean to you."

He stood and reached out as if to wipe a tear from my eye, hesitated, and dropped his hand. "You're a wise young lady—*Jessie*." I remember just how he said that, with that little break and then my name. Now I understand it, but then, of course, it puzzled me, as everything did, it now seems, in those days.

They found Sheriff Walkup's body crushed beneath the shrimp boat, which had nosed itself into the dunes of Whalehead and stuck. After sending the bodies of Garcie and Sheriff Walkup to the mainland for embalming they were brought back to Fortune Island for burial, Garcie in the black cemetery and Sheriff Walkup in the white, as was done in those days. There had been no time to make repairs, no time and no equipment to pull the shrimp boat out of the dunes, no time to clean up the cemeteries. The picket fences were gone. The stones of the older graves had sat underwater like lagan, keeping their places, naming their dead; but the newer graves had lost their flat markers. No worry, though, the few inhabitants of Fortune Island knew where their dead were buried.

The new graves waiting for their coffins held no puzzle but that of death. First we stood by Garcie's grave, then by Sheriff Walkup's, then I went and said a few words to my mother. I knew where she lay, even if the world did not. What could I say to the ground? Hold her tight? The ground would do that without understanding what it did. I wondered if the Traveller ever came here. I doubted it. And where was he now? He had left the island before the hurricane. He was probably somewhere at this very moment, shouting at people that they should believe, that they were evil and that that was why this awful storm had come. And that horrible man was all that I had left in this world. No, not all. Ruth and Tom Judas had come to join me at my mother's grave, Ruth, my benefactor, Tom, my savior. They just stood by, and that was enough. Then Ruth put her arm around my shoulders, and she never let go, at least not until I was a grown woman and could take care of myself.

IV.

With Garcie gone, the Traveller had to make new arrangements for me. I suggested Ruth.

"That painted heathen you're spending so much time with?"

"She's my friend," I said, "and she's already looking after me."

"Ain't she some kind of Yankee? Ain't she a Jew?"

"She's from Boston. She's real nice. She's rich and she's almost famous. She was the guest of honor at a party in Beaufort. The mayor was there and made a speech about her."

"Fancy that!" He didn't really care who watched out for me, he just had to get his shot glass full of meanness into it. So we trudged over to Ruth's house, him sweating and puffing with a hangover, and me not skipping but wanting to. It turned out just the way I wanted. He offered Ruth money to keep an eye on me when he was away, which was most of the time—he only came home to get drunk out of sight of anyone who might know him for a preacher—and Ruth did exactly what I knew she would do; she rejected his offer of money but told him that it would be a joy to her to keep an eye on me, that he need have no fear that I wasn't being looked after properly and that he could go about his business without hindrance.

Later he said, "Who's that uppity little skirt think she's talking to?" But he was happy enough to have unburdened himself of me on her, and so didn't question the situation any further, except to ask me how much money I thought she had. I told him I had no idea, which was true because I had no idea about money at all at the time. And, as Garcie would've said, that was another fork in the road.

Ruth had already begun educating me. She said I had an excellent brain—truly excellent. She said, "You're like a sponge. I've never seen anything like it. You appear to have a photographic memory and almost total recall." The fact that my brain was what she called excellent was more exciting to Ruth than it was to me. By the end of our first year together, she had me up to geometry and algebra and we were heading toward what she called "trig." Ruth said that it was good for her to go over a lot of this material because she had forgotten it.

"You don't use it," she said, "and it tends to fade away." She unwrapped the textbook she had bought in Wilmington. There it was—Trigonometry! And she had me reading Shakespeare. We acted the plays together. I found that I could remember whole passages without trying. Ruth said that I was "scary." I loved *Romeo and Juliet*. "How am I ever going to meet a boy on this island?"

"Plenty of time for that," Ruth said.

Ruth had taught me all about sex, but I couldn't understand where the force of love came from, though I could feel it. I could feel my love for Ruth. Ruth said that biology connected the two. That was my favorite subject, biology. How mussels mated! Those little whelks in their tube—was love involved somehow? If so, I couldn't tell how. It was clear to me that Romeo and Juliet wanted more than sex from each other, but what more did they want? I was learning so much so fast, sometimes it fell into a jumble, triangles and rectangles and arthropods and whelks and Romeo and Juliet and men and women in a heap on the dunes at night.

The times I hated most were the times when the Traveller was home and Ruth had to go to New York or to Boston to see her publisher or editor or on some other business. I would sneak out when the Traveller had drunk himself into a stupor and go to Ruth's—I had a key to her cottage now—and sit among her things where I was happy and could feel her near. But once, when the Traveller was away, and she had to go to New York, she took me with her, and oh heavens was that exciting! And I had thought that New York was so far away but on the airplane it only took a few hours. Ruth let me sit near the window so that I could see the geometry below, and it was just like in the textbooks, everything so different from down there, squared away and clean—the green field, a square house. And we went to the Museum of Modern Art in New York and there were the pictures that Ruth had on her walls at home—the cubists, the impressionists, VanGogh and Gauguin and my favorites the Renoirs with the beautiful ladies who looked like angels. Why did Picasso make ladies so ugly? Why did one lady have two faces? And we went to Radio City Music Hall and saw the Rockettes—the kicking, all in a row. I had never thought of such a thing. I had begun to realize that there was so much in the world that I had never thought of on my lonely island. But now I began to realize how lonely I had been growing up on that desolate dune. How could I have not known? But New York was overwhelming, and I got sick, and I was sick all the way back to

Fortune Island, and I didn't feel better until Ruth and I had tea together in her cottage, which felt like home to me.

Tom Judas had worked hard after the storm, saving what could be saved of the remaining dwellings on the Island. He continued to work for Mrs. Walkup and any-one else on the island who needed help. The church had been lifted off its footings, turned over, and sailed off into the sea like an empty ark, so a few of the fishermen along with Tom rebuilt it. He was much in demand. Carpenter, framer, plumber of wells, Tom could do it all. But most of that work was over. Now he was working on Ruth's cottage, fixing it up and adding a room. I thought of the new room as my own, but nobody said so: I just assumed. I spent a lot of time watching Tom work when I should have been studying. With his shirt off he looked very muscular. I liked to watch as his muscles stretched and contracted. He had become tan and even sunburned down his back. It seemed that he was always bending over something, hammering, sawing, or lifting. He glis-tened with sweat. I wanted him to talk to me.

"I have an excellent brain, you know," I said to him one day.

I couldn't understand why he burst out laughing.

"Do you think I'm funny?"

"No ma'am, I take you very seriously." But he kept on hammering at a plank. I couldn't help myself, but he made me think of biology. He could do so many things with those wonderful hands of his. He could play the guitar like nobody I ever heard before. Blues, he said; he said he played blues guitar, and sang songs that he wrote himself.

You send them out into this lonely life
They get a lonely woman for a wife
And then between them make
A hostage to fortune for the future's sake.

And you should have heard how he sang that one. He hit his guitar like a drum and then twanged it so a cat's fur would stand on end.

I learned he was an expert shot, too. Sometimes when the sea was quiet, when the surf was long and low, we could hear him out on the dunes popping Coke bottles. One day I went out there to join him and he showed me how to do it, how to load the clip in the pistol, pull the slide to get one in the chamber, how to aim and fire. I asked him if the gun was dangerous and he said No, not very, that it was just a little target pistol but don't go and point it at anyone because Yes, it could kill you if you were close up and got hit in the head by it. Always keep it pointed up, he said, away from people. I got pretty good at popping those bottles and he seemed to like having my company. Life had become exciting because I was learning so much about so many things; I, who had been alone with the whelklings for so long. Tom finally finished the work on Ruth's cottage. And it turned out that the extra room *was* for me. Ruth had it all gussied up with girl stuff, fluffy gingham curtains at the window, a bed with a thick patchwork quilt, some drawings I had made tacked up on the walls. I felt like a little rich girl, a princess.

And one day I heard Tom out there on the dunes popping those bottles and I went out to find him. He was leaning against a rock, his shirt off, a cigarette dangling from his mouth, taking pot shots at the bottles. He had told me that target shooting was his form of meditation, that he actually didn't think about the shooting but thought about other things when he practiced. "It's just something to do while I do my thinking," he had said. I often wondered what he was thinking about, but there was something about the way he told me that that indicated privacy, so I didn't ask. I thought that he did a lot of thinking though.

This time I went ahead and asked him.

"About the past, mostly," he said. "Sometimes about the future. Sometimes I think about you."

"Me? What do you think about me?"

"What a wonderful young girl you are."

That's what I was always thinking about him—I mean, what a wonderful man he was. I had to do something. I had to do something to show him how I felt. I was wearing a tissue-thin blouse Ruth had bought me in Wilmington. I knew if I got it wet, it would show that I wasn't a little girl anymore. I ran into the sea and came back to him and stood there, heaving my chest. He could see now that I was a woman, no doubt about it. But instead of reacting as I had hoped, he put his shirt over my shoulders and closed it in front and said, "I want you to come back to my shack with me. I have something to show you."

I didn't know what he had in mind, and, at first, it kind of scared me. But I could see sadness in his eyes, and I somehow realized that he was safe to be with. What had made me forget that for a moment? Myself, I guess. What I had been thinking about had caused me to worry, not anything he was doing. Anyway, when he led off, I followed and caught up and walked along beside him to the shack. It was a good long hot walk and we didn't talk. I had never been in his shack before. It was small, cramped, dark, full of stuff, a real mess, the kind men make when they don't care, when there are no women about.

He put the pistol in a drawer, saying he would clean it later. "But this is what I wanted to show you." He handed me a gold-framed photograph, one of those tinted pictures, of a woman and a little girl of about two or three.

"Is this your wife, Tom?"

"Yes, that's my wife. My ex-wife. She married someone else, but she's dead now."

"And the little girl is . . . the little girl . . ." I looked and looked and then I realized what I was looking at. The woman's hair was bunched in a snood, but I could see now that it was red hair, and the little girl had red hair too. I knew who it was before he said it.

"The baby is you, Jessie."

"And that's my mother. But how— Then you're—"

I stood there staring at him. I couldn't believe it.

"I'm your . . . dad, Jess. I thought . . . it was time for me to tell you."

"But my daddy has gray hair, everybody knows that. You can't be him!"

"I dyed it. I didn't want anyone here to recognize me. . . after all, I've been away a long long time." He sat at the table, not taking his eyes off me.

I threw my arms around his neck. "I knew it was you! Oh, I knew it was you!" A throb came up from my chest and I began to cry. Tom put his arms around me and patted my back. "Easy. Easy." he whispered.

"I knew it was you all the time," I said, sitting down across from him, "but I was afraid I might be wrong so I never said. I was too scared to think it. But there was something. . . Do you know how I mean, I mean—"

"I understand."

"But it's all coming true. It's coming true. Ruth—and now you!"

"Give me your hand, and let me explain," he said, reaching across the table, and I saw that he had tears in his blue eyes too. Tears for me? The tin roof of the shack began to drum with rain, as if in sympathy with us, and it became like a hollow, but steady rhythm above the noise of pounding water, almost echoing in the small enclosure, and I felt dizzy as I listened to him.

"I was young and foolish and believed I had to do something so that you and your mother wouldn't be dirt poor, and I committed a desperate and foolish act, an act that I have suffered for and have never stopped regretting, that I regret most perhaps at this very moment, when I have to tell you about it. Jessie, I'm full of shame and I want you to know that. And that stupid, youthful misdeed has kept me away from you all these years. It did the exact opposite of what I had hoped it would do. But I want you to know that I have never forgiven myself for it, for doing something that caused you to be without me during all those years when you needed me most." The rain came in bullets aimed at the roof. I was afraid the tin would puncture and we would die just at this moment, when I knew him, had him, could reach out and touch him.

"Your mother came to see me behind the Wall. She said that she had met someone who would take care of her. She wanted me to give her a divorce and sign the house over to her. I felt that it was the least that I could do. I thought you both needed that."

The roar of the rain made his voice seem far away, as if he were speaking to me on the telephone. "Later, I heard that your mom had died. All I could do then was to hope that your step-father, a man of God, I'd heard, would be good to you, love you as I did. I promised myself that as soon as I was freed, I'd come back here and see for myself how you were doing. If you were doing well, I would leave you alone, not interfere with your life, in any way. That's why I didn't want you to know who I was. I didn't want to be known. I just wanted to see. I had to see."

The drumming on the roof was beginning to soften, a cat's purr.

"I want to live with you," I said. My ears heard my creaky voice.

"I can't just take you away from Cogburn. Not just now. There are legal problems."

"Don't you want me?"

"I want nothing more in the world than that we be together. I love you with all my heart."

A thought jumped in at me, sudden as the rain had been. "I've got to tell Ruth. She'll be so . . . so *astounded!*"

"Ruth already knows, Jessie."

"She already knows?"

"I've told her the whole story."

"You told Ruth before you told me?"

"I wanted to know what she thought. Ruth and I have become pretty close, you know."

"Close? What does that mean? Close? Are you in love with her?"

"At this point, let's just say that we're friends."

"I know you're friends, but what kind of friends?"

I had green eyes—*green.* I couldn't help myself. Something had happened. The water was dropping outside. The shower was passing over. "I have to go and see Ruth," I said.

"But wait now—"

"No, I have to go and see Ruth." I'll come back, I said to myself, I'll come back.

"Wait, Jessie, I'll go with you."

"No! I want to see Ruth alone. I'll come back after I talk to Ruth. Wait for me. Don't come over. Don't go away. Stay right here."

"I'll clean the gun," he said, lighting a cigarette. The match flared up, etching his troubled face, his eyes dark hollows under the glinting strips of his corrugated brow. He was exercising a tortuous calculation, but plainly could come to no conclusion.

"Hurry back," he called after me.

"Yes, I'll come back," I said, plunging out the door. Most days it was water but today tiny diamonds dropped from the sky, glittering at every facet. How could the rain be mere water on a day like today? How could anything be what it tried to be? The wet sand jumped under my feet. It was alive! I made it dance but

I hurt it too. The atoms in my body were flying apart and crashing together. Something was going to heal, or break. It is just when everything is perfect that it explodes, for nature cannot bear perfection. Only an acceptable adaptation. If today was the happiest day of my life, I was also aware of the sun sinking out at sea. Ecstasy and terror. I punched the air and grabbed it as I ran toward Ruth's cottage. He had told Ruth before he had told me. Something was wrong with that. I wanted them both, I wanted them together, but I didn't want them without me. He should have explained everything to the two of us at once, for the three of us to share. But I knew what it was. I knew how they thought that they knew better. I had begun to see the treachery in grown-up thought, the kindly lies that only confused.

Ruth was working at the typewriter when I burst in. She stood up, seeing my confusion, my tear-stained eyes. For Ruth, I held no mystery. She read me as if what I thought ran across my forehead like the sign in Times Square.

"He's told you, hasn't he?"

"Yes. But he told you first. Why?"

"He wasn't sure how you'd take it. I told him that I thought you'd be fine. Was I wrong?"

"Oh Ruth!" I threw myself against her and she pulled me over to the couch where we sat together while I cried. It was all too much for me.

After a time, she said: "Were you angry because he told me first?"

"A little, I guess. Just a little hurt."

"I know, baby," she said. "It's an awful lot to take in, isn't it? All of a sudden you have a real father. But you suspected, didn't you?"

"I did. I don't know how but I did."

"I think you knew because you could tell that he loved you. You got it a little mixed up, though, maybe, didn't you?"

"I guess." I snuggled in her arms.

"Well, I have some more news for you, too," she said at last. "This is also pretty exciting. I got your high school GED test and your Sanford Binet back. I've brought you well beyond high school level and it looks like you're smarter than I am by a good twenty points. You're a gifted girl, Jessie. And you're going to have to go to school."

I jumped up from the couch. "What do you mean? Away?"

"I can send you to a very fine private school."

"But Tom—my *Dad*—I've just got him. He's here. I don't want to go away now."

"He thinks that if I'm willing to pay for your schooling, you should go. We've talked about it a good bit."

Now this scared me. "What school? Where?" I began to cry again, and Ruth pulled me back into her arms.

"I don't want to leave you, Ruth. I don't want to leave him."

I believed Ruth could do anything she wanted to. Hadn't she been able to get the academic tests that she told me were rarely allowed outside of institutional grounds? Now I was afraid she wanted to send me away.

I reached down into my desperation and came up with a counter argument. I sat up straight, facing her. "You can't make me go anywhere, you're not my mother. Are you and Tom—my dad—trying to get rid of me?"

"Sweetheart, why would we do that? We love you."

"So you can be alone together? Are you in love? Do you want to get rid of me? Am I in the way?"

I looked at her through my tears and saw that I had hurt her. I threw my arms around her neck. "Oh, I love you so much, Ruth. Please don't send me away."

"Let's just take our time, baby, and see what happens," she said. And that was it. A few days passed, then a few weeks, and there was no more talk of sending me away. I spent the mornings studying while Ruth worked on her book. Tom had taken over Sheriff Walkup's duties at the general store and usually joined us at dinnertime.

Ruth and Tom planned to take me into Wilmington the day before my fifteenth birthday, to celebrate. We had two rooms at the best hotel in town, the Cape Fear. The plan was for Ruth to take me shopping, and to outfit me like a young lady, "Like a debutante," Ruth said. She was so wealthy she made me feel like an heiress, just being with her. When she told Tom we were going shopping, he decided to tag along.

"I'd like to bear witness to the transformation," he said. And we set out in a gay mood. Being with Tom and Ruth was such fun, I had decided to forgive their occasional hand-holding, the looks that passed between them, which I could never quite understand. That day, at least, they were both focused on me. I had them both in my power, the power of my green eyes and red hair, even the power of my light tan freckles, which I urged to dazzle.

Those silly freckles have all faded away over the years, or have become an occasional brown mole here and there. Years of work in the sun have turned my fair, usually sun-burnt skin brown and creased, all the red has fallen out of my hair, and, as a result of chemo-therapy, much of my hair has been lost. But that day I shined, or so everyone said. The saleslady at Efird's said that I was beautiful.

"Those green eyes. . . she has got to wear mint-green. Let's try this," and she took down a floaty voile dress of mint-green, and, holding it up to my shoulders, said, "and I think white shoes and a white purse." Ruth told me to go into the dressing room and try it on.

I think that was the first time I had ever seen my-self from all sides and all the way around in back. Down to my underwear, I studied myself in the mirrors. Tall and thin I was, but I had nice long curves, more of a rump than I had realized, and in profile my breasts looked positively brazen in a new bra. My nose turned up more than I thought it did, but it was kind of cute, I thought, too. The saleslady handed me in a pair of white, open-toed pumps with heels at least two inches high. Of course I'd never owned a pair of high-heeled shoes before. I had to hobble, but I made my entrance. The first eyes I caught were Tom's. A father's eyes say, Look at my little girl. My emotions were turning in my stomach, this way and that, like snakes. I was happy and grateful and hurt all at once. Ruth said, "Oh, my dear, you look spellbinding." That was what she said, "spellbinding." The saleslady said, "She's fit for a grand party." Then I had a vanity attack, but with deep breathing, trying not to show what I was doing, my breasts heaving like that, I got myself back down to the almost right place, to where, I hoped, nothing was showing. "Not too bad, do you think?" I said, my ankles wobbling.

"Now all you need is a bouquet of flowers," said Tom. "I'll get you one before the day is over."

"It must be a special occasion," said the saleslady.

"Her birthday," said Ruth. "Tomorrow she'll be fifteen."

"Fifteen," Tom repeated in a wondering way.

"Fifteen, is it?" said the saleslady. "My compliments," she said to Ruth, "you look too impossibly young to have a fifteen year old. But looking at the two of you, I can see where she gets her looks. But where did the red hair come from?"

"Oh, she's not my daughter," Ruth said.

"Oh, I see," said the saleslady, taken aback. I noticed her curiosity. I suppose we did seem an odd threesome, but, momentarily at least, we were a very happy threesome.

Outside, Ruth told Tom that she was taking me to have a manicure and a pedicure and a permanent wave, so he might as well busy himself elsewhere. He said he would go and get the flowers and a few other things and meet us back at the hotel. I was so excited that I thought I actually saw some of my freckles jump off my arms. Well, I was seeing spots before my eyes, but my wobbling ankles really hurt. It was a hot day and I think they were beginning to swell. Or had my new nylons bunched? I felt so tall, wobbling along beside Ruth in my new heels. She was five six or seven and I swear I was looking down at her.

The Cape Fear Hotel had one of the best restaurants in Wilmington, or so Ruth said. I was proud of my newly-shaped and pink painted fingernails and kept holding them in view of the youngish waiter to see if I could detect a reaction, but I guess he had seen a lot of nails on a lot of girls because he was all polite business. He switched from a soft cultured southern accent to French—especially when he spoke directly to Ruth, who answered him in French, some of which I could understand—if only they had slowed down—coq au vin—and back to "Will the gentleman approve the wine?" Tom knew what to do, which surprised me. He took a sip and said, "Fine" and the waiter poured. Tom had given me flowers to wear and for a birthday present a silver necklace with a locket containing a picture of himself and a picture of Ruth.

"Oh, I just love it," I told him, thinking right away that I might replace Ruth's picture with my own. That made me feel so guilty, I felt like crying. I took Ruth's hand and said, "I love you, Ruth." Her big dark eyes grew glassy and she turned quickly to say something to Tom. He looked kind of soppy too. Gosh, we were all just looking so sad, I had to do something. "I love all my gifts," I said. "Thank you. Thank you both so much."

"But tomorrow's the real party," Tom said, brightening.

"We're going to show you the town," Ruth said. "There's a fair on the outskirts. Would you like to go to the fair?"

"We'll have a picture taken of the three of us," Tom said, "to mark the occasion." I was so happy that night. I never wanted to leave them, but I couldn't help feeling that somehow Ruth was stealing my dad from me, or was it that Tom was stealing Ruth from me?

Ruth and I had a room to ourselves and Tom had a room down the hall. In 1957, and especially in a good hotel in the south, hanky-panky was frowned on, at least openly. Certainly there were hotels where things went on, but not in the Cape Fear. The unnoticed and all-seeing bellhops kept the nightclerks posted. In such a hotel, house detectives were not uncommon. If progress is movement in a desirable direction, I am dumb to say where we have got to in the year 2000. If I outlast this cancer by a few more years, I'll be content, but I have little desire to see what's coming much ahead. Biology has been my field and my life, but I'm concerned as to where it is going.

Nevertheless, you must have agriculture before you can have high culture and you must have biology before you can have love, so I reach for faith out of thin air, like Shakespeare's poet, or like his madman. But that night Ruth and I climbed into the softest bed I had ever—ever what? It was beyond my dreams. It was a cloud in the heaven I even then doubted, yet that bed made me believe in it. At first, I was like the girl with visions of sugar plums dancing in her head; but I awoke from a sweet, forgotten dream of warmth to find the warmth and then the source of the warmth missing.

"Ruth?" I got up and went to look in the bathroom. No Ruth. I felt a bit frightened. Something must be wrong. I checked the clock, thinking that I'd overslept, but it was just one o'clock in the morning. She must have gone to Tom's room. But what for? What had happened? I put my raincoat over my pajamas and stepped out into the carpeted, ornate hall. One could see through the transoms, light or no light in the rooms. A few were lighted. There was a long dark wall table with a vase of flowers and a straight chair at each end, backs to the wall. Soft night lights—everything white and gold. The thick gold carpet tickled my feet. I came to Tom's door, a few doors down from ours, and I heard voices over the transom, which glowed with soft light. I listened but could not make out what was being said. All I could hear was groans, or maybe moans. Was Tom hurt? I started to knock, but something warned me not to, an instinct, a primitive sense, warning of privacy, secrecy. If they had needed me, they would have awakened me, I reasoned. But what was it? I tried to see through the keyhole, but the key must have been in the lock and I could see nothing but shadow and a blurry wire of light, indicating somehow taboo, privacy, secrecy, saying that what was happening inside was not for me to know. But the moans and groans were growing in intensity, and I was afraid.

I went back down the hall and got one of the straight chairs and brought it back to the door and stood up on it and could just see over the top of the door, through the open transom. Ruth and Tom were naked on the bed, Ruth straddling him and rocking and him heaving, and I felt faint. Woozy. But above all, I didn't want them to know I was there. I got down and took the chair and put it back in its place and went to my room, trying to catch my breath. I threw up my dinner in the toilet, flushed it, closed the lid, and sat there, trying to get things in order. They are lovers! Or was it just biology? Did they have to do this on my birthday? My beloved ones were like animals! I had dreamed of love, but not like that, not like what I'd seen. My heart was not right, and the snakes in my stomach uncoiled and came up through my windpipe and I screamed. I whirled around the bathroom, smashing things. Oh, had anybody heard? I listened. Nothing. I felt trapped. I had to get out into the street, into the cool night air. I dressed myself in my new clothes, heels and all. I smeared lipstick on, and pushed my new permanent into place, took the key, and found the elevator. The doors slid open.

"Down?" said the bellhop, holding the handcrank, and down and out I went, one thought in my mind: "I hate them! I hate them!"

Their naked image was all I could see. I felt like a green-eyed monster. Not wanted, shut out! I wanted to kill them. No, I didn't! I loved them. I hobbled along in my high heels and my Sunday dress feeling like a freak of some kind. What was I doing? Where was I going? Where could I go? Well, the answer to that one came quickly enough. I hadn't gone a block before a car pulled up alongside me. There were two sailors in it. "Where you going, baby?"

"Where are you two going?"

"Just cruising. Want to cruise?"

I got in the back seat. The sailor who was driving said, "Back at base, they call me Devil and him Angel. What do we call you?"

"It's my birthday," I said. I don't know why I said it, it just popped out.

"Okay, we'll call you birthday girl, okay?" Devil had done all the talking so far. Angel sat on the passenger side and looked, I thought, kind of forlorn.

"Here," said Devil, "take a snort of this," and he handed me back a bottle of whiskey in a brown paper bag. "It's a happy birthday drink."

"You don't look old enough to drink," said Angel.

"She looks plenty old to me," said Devil.

Devil seemed older than Angel, who seemed closer to my age. If people really did call them Devil and Angel I could see why. Devil was dark and tough-looking and sounded like a yankee, and Angel was blond and had a sweet face, really angelic, as I could see when he turned to talk. "Don't drink so much of that," Angel said.

The whiskey was like fire and my first impulse was to spit it out, but I gripped myself and swallowed, feeling it boil down into my guts.

"Good, eh?" said Devil. "Happy birthday to you!"

"Oh," I said, pulling the bottle away, "it's like fire."

"Oh, that stuff ain't nothin'," said Devil. "I'm going to drive us out to a place I know where they got a still and a place to drink white lightning—and you can dance there too. Like to dance, Birthday Girl?"

"Listen," said Angel, "how old are you?"

"Eighteen," I lied.

"Are you sure, because you don't look eighteen. I got an eighteen year old sister and she looks a lot older 'an you."

"What you talking about?" said Devil. "You saw how tall she is!"

"But look at her face."

"Looks pretty good to me."

Something like that—because I couldn't tell for certain what they were saying. I didn't realize it, but I was getting drunk, another entirely new experience for me.

"Go ahead," Devil would say, "have another drink," and I heeded his encouragement, ultimately getting down at least half a pint of whiskey. And oh, the warmth, the sweet ease of it! For the time-being the ugly image of Tom and Ruth faded from view, the beautiful, sweet face of Angel turned to me and kept on turning. Then I saw that we were out in the woods and I began to get scared. "You better let me out," I said.

"Let her out," Angel said. "Let us both out. I don't want to go to any still, I don't even drink."

"Aw, come on," said Devil.

"No, let us out!"

"Well, shee-it!" Devil slowed the car and pulled over. "Go ahead, but you're gonna miss one hell of a time." We got out—Angel had to steady me—and Devil roared off honking his horn.

There we stood, out on this narrow country road with a partial roof of rainy-sounding leaves coming from both sides and almost meeting above us in the middle, soft moonlight floating down through the clouds. The soft hoot of an owl made it spooky.

"How far are we from town?" I asked.

"Not far," said Angel, "if we don't get lost."

"Do you know the way?"

"I think so. Come on."

My ankles hurt. I slipped off my shoes and walked in my stockinged feet. To make conversation, I asked about Devil. "Is your friend really bad?"

"Oh, you mean that Devil stuff. His name is Devlin, so they started calling him Devil. He tries to be a tough guy, because he's from Boston."

"I know somebody from Boston. She's my best friend in fact."

"Devlin's going to get himself in trouble with his drinking, though. That's something we all should be careful of, that drinking. I've known it to bring ruin on people, members of my own family, even. I don't drink none at all. Don't smoke, neither."

"Is that why they call you Angel?"

"My name's Johnny Engels—that's where that comes from. What's yours—your name?"

"Jessie McQueen."

"That's a nice name. What's got you so ripped up tonight, miss? You look like you been to a party—did you have a fight with somebody or did somebody walk out on you or did you walk out on somebody else? We saw you come storming out of the Cape Fear Hotel. Shucks, I couldn't afford to check in there even for one night. Heck, a half a night! And you in that beautiful dress—what happened?"

The trees seemed to be moving backwards, with all their shadows and moon-patches, receding behind us. I felt drunk, but clearing up a bit, holding my own, I thought. What makes that night so vivid is that it was the last night, the tail end of my happiness, which already seemed like a long-ago dream.

"Something happened that made me hate the two people that I loved best in the world, that's what happened. Let's stop for a minute, my ankles hurt." I sat down by the side of the road, and leaned against a tree. "Look at them, they're all swollen."

"Sure looks like."

"How old are you, Angel?"

"Eighteen."

"Angel, would you do me a favor?"

"Sure. What?"

"Kiss me."

He made a little tight smile, squinted his eyes, and tilted his head. It was a questioning, good-humored look. "What? Just like that?"

"Like this," I said, and, grabbing his ears in my hands, I kissed him hard on the mouth and held on until he shook me off. "What's the matter?"

I thought any boy would respond with passion, but not Angel.

"Now that's what I mean about the alcohol," he said. "We're going to get ourselves into all kinds of trouble."

"I'm a virgin," I said. "Don't you want me?"

"Oh my, yes, course I do. But you don't really want to do this out here like this. It's because you've been drinking. And let me tell you something. There's nothing wrong with being a virgin. Why, every man wants his bride to be a virgin, and he should be a virgin too, so that they know no other forever always until death do them part."

"Angel, you're a virgin, too, is that it?"

"Keeping myself for the future Mrs. Engels, miss. And I got me sisters and I hope they are keeping themselves too. Expect they are."

"Come on," I said, "walk me back to the hotel."

"But now which way do we go?" Angel said to himself. "See up yonder—there's a fork there."

"There's more glow over left," I said.

"That's probably the town."

Do I imagine all this? Did this interlude develop in my imagination over the near half century since whatever happened on that road that night happened? I remember it almost word for word as if it had happened yesterday, but did I pose the words, did I develop the events? I can't help myself. This is what I remember, and this: that I wanted him so badly that my body ached; that I tried to think of a way to get him to come to my room; that I tried this: "If I'm left alone, I may kill myself. I mean it. I have nothing to live for anymore. I have been . . . betrayed."

"Don't say that, miss." The poor boy looked worried. "Now look, miss Jessie, I can't get into that hotel. There's a desk clerk, for sure, watches everbody comes and goes."

"I could go in first, and you come in and rent a room and then come to my room and sit with me."

"A room in a place like that would cost me my pay, and I don't have much of that left anyway."

"I have money." I pushed twenty-five dollars on him, money which Ruth had given me for anything I wanted—well, I wanted Angel.

"No, miss, I can't take your money."

"Not even to save my life?"

He puzzled.

"Suppose you read in the papers tomorrow that a young girl jumped from the window of the Cape Fear Hotel, then you'll be sorry that you didn't take the money and save her, won't you?"

"Well—I suppose—"

I won; he took the money.

Tangled laundry, my emotions, wet and steamy, and I couldn't pull a shirt from a towel. Tom and Ruth had behaved like animals, and I hated them for it, but I wanted to do the same thing with Angel, in part to get even with Tom and Ruth, in part because Angel was just about the first boy I had ever been with in any old way at all. He was the first boy I had ever kissed. That must seem impossible to some, but I am the only Jessie, wild girl of Fortune Island, and I know it to be true. I wanted to be under that boy and over Tom and Ruth, I wanted to outdo them at their own dirty game and I wanted to know how it felt to be made love to—what biology felt like—and maybe, for a brief instant, I was really in love.

I passed the door of Tom's room, where Ruth and Tom must lay now in an exhausted doze, and went to my room and set what I thought would be the perfect trap. I stripped down to my skin and waited for Angel.

Soon enough came a quiet knock. I opened the door, staying behind it, and let him in. Then, as he stood trying to adjust to the one endtable light I had left on, I slammed the door and put a chair under the knob. When Angel turned and saw me naked before him, he stepped back like he'd been shot. He even reached for his heart, as if to be certain that it was there and beating, or maybe to stop it from beating so wildly, to hold it still. I threw myself at him and he fell backwards onto the rumpled bed.

"Oh my Lord," he said, "miss, what are you doing?" I didn't know exactly—several things at once, I'd say now. But before anything could be sorted out, Ruth was at the door, trying to get in, shaking the knob, inching the door open. Angel found his way out from under me and ran to the door, as if for help. Then I heard Ruth, "Jessie! Why is this door jammed?" And Angel, "I'll get it open, ma'am." And Ruth again, "Who is that? Open this door! Jessie!" And Angel, "I didn't do anything, honest, as God is my witness." And me, "You jerk!"

Then Tom's voice, "Open this door, dammit!"

"Yes, sir. But you see the harder you push the harder it is for me to open it."

"Who in hell are you?"

"Nobody, sir—just a sailor."

"What are you doing in there?" That was Ruth.

The door flew open. Tom stepped in, saw me, and backed out. Ruth replaced him. "Get your clothes on, young lady."

"That girl is under age," Tom shouted from the hall. "If you've laid a hand on her—"

"God in heaven may strike me dead, sir, if I—"

"Or I'll strike you dead," said Tom.

Ruth pushed Angel out into the hall. "Tom, take this boy down to your room and talk to him."

Tom grabbed the young sailor by the arm. "Come on, boy."

"Did he lay a hand on you?"

"He didn't have a chance. But I wanted him to."

"You what?"

"Like you and Tom."

"Tom and I? I just went down the hall to see—"

"I saw you—through the transom."

"Oh, honey, no!"

"You're going to send me away to school so you can have him for yourself!"

"Here, put something on. You don't understand."

"All I need to know, you bitch!"

And Ruth knocked me across the bed with a roundhouse right. "Oh, my God," she said—"I'm sorry, baby."

"I hate you! I hate Tom! I don't know which one of you I hate the most. I hate you both!"

After due explanation, I suppose, Angel was set free to pursue his quest for a virginal bride. I finally fell into a troubled sleep, awakening several times to find Ruth, pillow-propped, holding me in her arms. Finally I went into a deeper sleep that lasted until noon. When I woke, I realized that I was truly fifteen. Today was my birthday. Of course the big day we, or Tom and Ruth, had planned was not to be. They had been busy arranging for a different kind of day while I slept. Ruth had hired a fisherman who owned a cabin cruiser, really not much more than a motor launch, to take us back to Fortune Island. She'd found Mr. Masefield on the Wilmington docks, advised by others that he was a man who liked the isolation of the island and was always pleased to have an excuse to cross Pamlico and put up on the island for a day or two of fishing.

Tom and Ruth looked sad, maybe ashamed, and I felt horrible, ugly and mean. Ruth had bought me a birthday cake and she held it in her lap in the launch like a precious artifact. She stared at it, not looking up for the whole time it took to get to the tail-end of the island. Tom talked to Mr. Masefield and smoked cigarette after cigarette. I had never seen him chain-smoke before. Now I can only imagine what he was thinking; then I couldn't imagine at all. Whatever I thought he was thinking was unquestionably wrong, for I was seeing all this through the eyes of someone deliberately misled, albeit for my own good, as others understood that good. Later, when Ruth thought I was mature enough to understand, she tried to explain to me that Tom, already so full of guilt, now felt worse than ever, felt that he had let me down in the worse way possible. This was the man to whom I owed my very life.

He had saved me from drowning during the hurricane; had come out to the most isolated area of the island at the height of the surge in that little skiff to save all of us, Ruth, Garcie, and myself, and then had actually pulled me from the flood; had appeared, like a guardian angel, out of nowhere. I owed him my life. Why couldn't I simply accept the fact that he and Ruth were in love, that they saw us as a family, that neither of them would have excluded me for any imaginable reason—that they loved me, Tom in his way and Ruth in hers. But I sat there, with one isolation inside another like a Chinese box of isolations, with sullen pride immingled with fear and watched the waves from the wakes of boats out of sight follow one another, this way and that, apparently pointlessly, and finally the darkness in me spread to the sky and it began to rain and Pamlico Sound roughened and frothed.

Ruth tried again at her cottage. She made coffee and put candles on the cake and lit them and brought it to the table singing "Happy Birthday," but I would have none of it.

"Betrayers!" I cried, melodramatically. "You both want to get rid of me so that you can have each other without being bothered with me." It was the first time I had spoken since Wilmington and I could see that my words came as a great disappointment. Tom shook his head.

"If you only knew," he said.

"You two want to send me away. That's what it is."

"No, no, no, no," Tom said, shaking his head.

"What Tom is trying to say is—"

"You just want to be through with me and have him to yourself."

"Baby, Tom and I love each other."

"Then why did you stop me with Angel? Don't you want me to ever be in love?"

"Because you're too young," said Tom.

"You could ruin your life," said Ruth. "You have a brighter future than you can imagine, I promise you."

"Where were either one of you when I was alone on this damned island? You have no right to try to run my life now."

"Come on," said Ruth, "blow out your candles. Let's try to have a little party together."

"Here's how I'll blow them out," I said, opening the door to the wind and rain. They flickered, and blew out. Ruth said there was no use in my behaving like a brat. She said she was tired and had to get some rest. She tried to kiss me but I moved aside. I went in my room and played possum. Pretty soon I heard Ruth and Tom go in Ruth's bedroom and close the door. I couldn't control my emotions; I felt strange, as if I were watching myself from somewhere up in the night sky.

I ran all the way to what should have been my house but which was now the Traveller's. I was still wearing my mint-green Sunday dress—but it was wet and wrinkled now—and my hair was all in wet ringlets. I had forgotten to wipe the lipstick from my mouth. I burst in the door.

The Traveller sat with bottle at elbow. He looked up from his Bible and said, "Painted woman! I've been back since yesterday. I suppose you were out somewhere with that Jew bitch. Do you know that she paid me two-thousand dollars for you?"

I sat down across from him, panting, trying to catch my breath. "What do you mean?"

"She bought my signature. I signed you away to her in case of my death. Guardianship, it's called."

"Ruth paid you two-thousand dollars for me?"

"What I said."

"She must love me," I said, "at least two-thousand dollar's worth.".

"Same as buying a slave, ain't it? Nobody loves a slave."

"She'd never think of me as a slave, I know that."

He took a long drink. "Well, what do you think, think I don't love you?"

"You! You don't love anything or anyone."

"I love God."

"You love being God."

"Well—" he lurched up. "Look at you," he said. "Like a grownup woman, with that paint on your face and that dress—where'd you get that? Never mind, I know. You look just like your red-headed mother, the whore of Wilmington. He leaned with both hands on the table and moved hand over hand around it toward me. I jumped up and moved away. "Come here," he said. "Don't run away. Give me a kiss. A father has a right to kiss his daughter, doesn't he?"

"You're not my father! I have a real father!"

"No, I'm not and yes, you do, and he's a criminal in the Central Prison in Raleigh. Or maybe he's dead. I don't keep up with such people. Or maybe he's done out. Maybe he's been out."

"My father's right here on Fortune Island."

"Sure he is—me—I'm here!"

I was afraid he was going to grab at me, as he had often done of late. I kept moving away from him but then I saw that he had me trapped. He was between me and the door. "Now you leave me alone," I said. But he got a drunken leer on his face and moved toward me. I was being backed to the attic door. There was no place to go but up. I ran up the stairs and looked for something in the dark to hit him with if he came up after me. But he was there already, on the top step. I kicked at him, to keep him from coming up, but he fended off my kicks and kept on coming toward me, looming in the light from below. Then he swung out to grab me or to hit me and I caught the blow on my cheek and fell to floor and he was on top of me, pulling at my dress. One arm was pinned beneath me and with the other I flailed his face, neck, shoulders over and over and over and over and oh—oh God!

Finally, he left me there, broken open, used up. I heard him half fall down the stairs to the main room. I heard the bottle crash. In a little while I heard the door slam, then slam again and again, wind-caught. I lay there in the dark and listened to the door slam for what seemed hours. He had ripped my beautiful Sunday dress up the front. It didn't matter. It was just a rag now. Blood has a metallic smell. Biology was not always beautiful, a miracle. Where was love? Why hadn't it been Angel? I lay there in the dark and reached out on the floor around me, looking for something. What was I looking for? My locket! I felt for my locket and it was there. Oh Ruth. Tom. This was my birthday. I was grown now, wasn't I? The Traveller had his own little skiff and I wondered if he had gone off to the mainland on it, had just decided to leave me here in the attic by myself with nothing but damp books, musty boxes. I reached out and felt around for my father's books that had started me reading so long ago. I just lay there, feeling how worthless I was, and for the first time I could guess at my mother's life with the Traveller, how he must have made her feel, weak sinner that she was. No wonder she threw herself into the sea. I should go down to the shore and throw myself in, for I'm nothing now, less than nothing. I can't offer myself to anyone ever again. There will never be love of that kind in me for anyone after this. In and out I went, sleeping, thinking, sleeping, the door downstairs banging, until a candle-glow of light began to shape and frame the small window at the back end of the attic, a patch of tarnished silver.

Somebody got up and left me there. I had been split in two. I stayed where I was, looking up at the dark insides of the attic, and the other went to the landing. Which was I? The one at the landing left the other on the floor in the attic and descended, going where? Out! Away! But not to Ruth's, not to Tom's. They must never see me again. I was leaving Jessie McQueen in the attic with her books, her father's books, her grandmother's books. I was someone else, a new and different creature.

Him! He lay at the bottom of the stairs, his right leg twisted up under him, as in a wild dance step. I saw that the door was banging still, taken by the wind. He hadn't left; he had been here all night, sleeping off his alcohol, dreaming God knew what horrible dreams, because it wasn't in him to have sweet ones. His must have been full of demons, for he never saw a good thing; everything was sad and bad for the Traveller. I couldn't get out without stepping on him. I was barefoot and doubted if he would feel it. I jumped over him, stepping once lightly on his back, but he caught me by an ankle and kept me there.

"I fell down the stairs," he mumbled. "Help me to the cot. You pull and I'll push with my good leg."

"So you're awake."

"Off and on all night. I'm in terrible pain. I think I broke my ankle."

"Don't you remember what you did last night?" I shouted, kicking him.

"All I've ever done to you is to take good care of you after your mother died. I remember there was a tramp came in here last night that looked like your mother, a painted whore from Wilmington, picked up and assaulted by some sailors, no doubt. I am the man who married Magdalene."

"God, you're still drunk."

"Can't be. Hurts too much. Get me to the cot."

If he had let go of me once I would have fled, but he managed to keep a grip on me somewhere, my arm, my wrist, my ankles, as I dragged him and he kicked with his good leg over to the cot and pulled himself up on it.

"That's better," he said, settling. "Put something under that foot."

I pushed a chair over to him and lifted his bad leg up on it. I felt cold as ice. He pulled up his trouser leg and we saw that the leg was badly swollen and red. "Get me a bottle of whiskey from the cupboard. I've got to kill the pain." I got it.

"Why should I help you? You. . ." I stomped to the door and made it stop slamming.

"Because I'm your father and you must honor me."

"After last night? And since when have you been any kind of father to me? I've hated you since before I knew what hate was."

"You keep talking about last night. Nothing happened last night but that I fell down the stairs."

"Why are your pants open and half way down, old man? What do you think you were doing up in the attic?"

He took a long chug from his bottle. "I was looking for you. You're never here when I come home. I want you to be here. I demand that you be here, do you hear me?"

"I never know when you're coming home. How am I supposed to know? But you, damn you, you're not going to get away with what you did this time. Look at me, I'm bruises from head to foot. You raped me . . . you monster. . . monster!"

"Don't you ever say a thing like that again, girly, or you'll find yourself in big trouble. I'm a preacher of God, do you hear?"

"Ruth says you're a drunken con-man, a crook who takes advantage of poor stupid people. Why hasn't the church in the village ever asked you to preach there? Why do you have to go and find these crazy little churches in the back woods? That's what Ruth says. And Garcie said the same thing." I was breathless.

"Garcie! An ignorant nigger and a Jew bitch!"

"You talked my mother into divorcing my father when he was in trouble. That's how you got this house. And now you've sold me to Ruth like a slave being sold at market."

"It's for your own good. Suppose I had died falling down those stairs—well, there'd be somebody to look after you."

"But you made her pay you."

"Why shouldn't I get some of the money back that it cost me to raise you up? There's been a lot of expenses. Now I'm in pain." He winced. "The whiskey helps but it's not going to stop it. You got to go into the village and get somebody out here to help me, maybe get me over to Beaufort to a doctor."

"You can't walk out on me this time, can you? You're trapped here."

"You can see that; now get going!"

“I’ll take my own sweet time,” I said, using a phrase of Ruth’s. “The longer you hurt the better.”

“A curse on you, girl, a curse on you.”

Of course there was a curse on me, and I couldn’t have been more keenly aware of it. The girl in the attic reached out to touch what was left of her childhood. The girl down here reached out for a weapon. Possession? Derangement? Dislocation? Someone else was changing my clothes out in back of the house in the rain. Someone else took my lovely mint-green dress that was nothing now but a rag and stuffed it in the cave at the back of the house, the cave I could no longer squeeze into, the little cave half flooded with rain, the wet blanket, and now my beautiful birthday dress in tatters down that rabbit hole. I must have been the size of a rabbit to have ever fitted into that hole, to have hidden there as I so often did. Someone else put on jeans and a shirt and raincoat and hat and trudged off in the lightening rain toward the village. Jesse McQueen was dead.

Who—whom had I become? Someone else looked out of my eyes. Someone else heard the gulls cry. Another face felt the rain. Someone else returned Mrs. Walkup’s wave and someone else saw the General Store, and someone else turned beside it and went on to the shack behind it. The new person knew that Tom would still be with Ruth. The new person knew that the pistol would be in the place, in the dresser drawer, Tom’s target pistol, which he had taught Jessie McQueen to shoot. This new person, I, I knew that, if I looked, I would find the pistol, and I did.

How small am I, this new person? Smaller than a snail. Smaller than a bug, to be stepped on. Everyone is gone from my sight. I have no one, no other. They are all gone. Yesterday is gone. Everything is gone but the one thing, the monster. The monster has always been there and the monster will always be there, no matter which tyne of the fork you take. I am an unclean and worthless creature. I know that now. I am removed. I am someone other than who I once was walking with the pistol in my pocket as the rain pauses, stops, and the sun comes out. I am close now. I am near the door.

I pull the door open and step in and shut the door.

"There you are! Did you get some help?"

"I'm here to help," I said. "Just like when I was a little girl and you fell down."

"What's the matter with you? You don't look right."

"No. I don't feel like myself. Myself must have died."

"What are you jawing about, girl. Get me some help." He raised the bottle to his lips in such a familiar gesture—I had an album of pictures of that gesture, some dating back to my earliest memories. I saw the Liberty ships in Wilmington, the cypress trees behind them. I could still feel the sting on my cheeks from his wet-handed slaps across my face. I could still see the lady, sympathetic, making a motion for me to wipe my tears. I took out the pistol, aimed, and shot. "You raped me," I whispered, with a deep, stranger's voice.

He sat there with a stunned expression on his face, but not what I expected. I saw that there was blood near his left shoulder.

"Why you crazy little bitch, you shot me." He set the bottle in his lap and felt his shoulder. "Damnation," he said, "that smarts something fierce. What is that thing? A twenty-two? Where'd you get it?"

I shot him again. It hit him in the side of the stomach, by the liver.

"Oh my God!" he cried, leaning forward.

I felt faint, dots dancing before my eyes. I went to the table and sat down at his place, where he always sat, where I could look straight at him.

"You better think what you're doing, girl," he said. I could see now that he was feeling a lot of pain. I held the butt of the pistol on the table to steady it, and shot him again. The bottle in his lap shattered. He screamed. His scream just sounded like something he did at his sermons. He was always screaming at people. I pulled the trigger again, and waited. He was quiet this time, his eyes closed. There was a lot of blood all over him. I sat there waiting for something to happen. Then he moaned. I pulled the trigger—pop, pop, pop.

She was almost sure that he was dead, whoever she was. Minutes passed.

Someone was knocking. I had to find myself. I had to answer. Then I heard Ruth: "Is anyone there? Jessie?"

"Hello," called Tom, knocking harder at the door.

"I'm here," I called, suddenly afraid they would leave me alone with the Traveller, "I'm here. Wait. I'll open the door." I felt as if the body I had left in the attic had rejoined me. I was inside of myself again, terrified, horrified, alone. I left the gun on the table and scrambled to the door. Ruth and Tom stood waiting. I spread my arms to collect their reality. Now all of that icy calm I had felt had gone out of me. They told me later that I was hysterical, that I spoke incoherently, that I was sobbing and choking and that my knees went out from under me as I tried to tell them what happened. Ruth told me that Tom caught me up and carried me into the room. If this happened as I have been told, I have no memory of it. Ruth found another bottle of whiskey and made me drink some of it. I remember how I couldn't get my breath, how I was afraid that I might die there and then for lack of air, like a fish out of a tank. Then I heard what Ruth and Tom were saying.

"Is he alive?" I heard Ruth say. "I'll go and get help."

Tom said that the Traveller was dead. I distinctly heard him say, "He's dead." Dead, dead, dead. But that's not what I heard him say a few minutes later. I still don't know for certain what to believe about that, because I was sure I heard him say, "He's dead." I am almost sure I heard him say that. I think that's what he said. Between choking and sobbing and gulping air I said, "He . . . raped me. Bruises—look at my arms."

They looked at me with faces filled with horror.

"Oh, no, baby," Ruth said in a whisper, sitting down beside me, hugging me, "oh, no, baby."

"This is all my fault," said Tom. "I've done it again—bringing that stupid pistol to the island. I'm a damned felon. I shouldn't have had the damned thing anyway."

Ruth's face had changed from the knitted brow of horror to wide-eyed amazement. "Your fault? How can it be your fault?"

"I should have got her out of here, Ruth, somehow. This is my fault. All of it is my fault. My poor wife's suicide, the life Jessie must have had with this brute, all of this is my fault, mine, and I'm not going to let her take the blame for what I've done, for my failure—for my mistakes. The blame for this is mine!"

"But Tom—" Ruth started.

"No buts. Please, Ruth, no buts!" He waved his hands wildly in a desperate attempt to explain himself. "Jessie didn't do this. *I* did it. As sure as if I'd pulled the trigger. You hear?" He went to the table and picked up the gun. "Hear him moaning? He's alive."

Out of some tunnel, I heard my echoing voice: "You said he was dead."

"He's not dead!" Tom yelled, startling the room with his vehemence.

"Then we can get him to the mainland," Ruth said, "to the hospital."

"He'd never make it. Turn away. Both of you. I want to see if he's got a pulse."

"What are you going to do?" Ruth said.

"Turn away," Tom shouted. "Jessie, turn away." We did as we were told.

There was a shot. Ruth was holding me and I could feel her shudder. Then we looked. At first I couldn't see anything different, but then I saw a small black hole in the Traveller's forehead. Tom stepped in front of the body and when he stepped away there was a trickle of blood from the hole. How did it get there?

"See," Tom said, "he was alive. You see the blood? I killed him."

Ruth said, "Are you sure, Tom—I mean, you want to do this, this way? It'll be the end of us."

"Us? What about her? The least she'd get is reform school until she's twenty-one. This wasn't self-defense. They'll call it premeditated. I don't want to spoil her life. Haven't I done enough to spoil it already? I came back here to watch over her and I've messed that up, but this time I'm going to make things come out right."

"Of course—you're right. Whatever you say."

"I'll probably get second degree. I could be out—well, I won't be in forever. I must have a solemn oath from both of you. You must promise on whatever you hold sacred that you don't know anything about this."

He spoke quickly and softly now, almost whispering. "It was something between him and me and I'll be sitting here holding the gun when they come. If I admit to it, nobody'll look any further. That's the story. You must promise me never to tell another. Do you promise? Do you promise? Do you promise? Do you swear?"

"If you want it to be this way," said Ruth, "Jessie and I promise you. Ruth shook me gently. "Your dad's right. Do you hear, Jessie? Do you promise?"

"I promise," I said, Ruth squeezing it out of me.

"We promise," Ruth said.

"There's more," said Tom. "Ruth, I want you to take Jessie and get to Boston as soon as you can. Get Masefield to take you back to Wilmington. He won't be far off. You can find him. He might be asleep on his boat. Get him and get to Wilmington and get to Boston. And don't contact me. Not a word. Do you understand? Not a word!"

"Oh God, Tom," said Ruth, "No!"

"I don't want you to contact me in any way. Do you swear?"

Ruth shook her head slowly from side to side and her big dark eyes were so full of sorrow that I had to look away. She said, in a broken voice, "I—I swear."

"Look," Tom said, "It's not the end. We'll be together again. All of us. Just a matter of time." He got up and took Ruth in his arms and kissed her, then me. He gave me a long look.

"Now take her and go. I want you in Boston by tomorrow. That's the best thing you can do for me. For all of us."

"I'll do it," said Ruth. "You know you can depend on me."

He gave Ruth a rueful smile. "When I feel you're safely gone, I'll go and get someone and tell them—how I hated the son-of-a-bitch, how I shot him, and that's all I am going to say to anyone, ever. Even if they wanted to prove differently, which they won't, because I'll make their case for them, even if they wanted to prove differently, they couldn't."

And, David, that promise cost you your father. Of course, he didn't know about you then, none of us did. But this is why I ask your forgiveness, and why I insisted on bearing the name Judas, because I allowed him to sacrifice himself, and, in doing so, betrayed you even before you were born. But Ruth and I did exactly what your father—and my father—ordered us to do. Ruth gave me pills to take, and she kept me sedated enough to follow her like a zombie, or be dragged by her, until we got off the airplane in Boston. Between the sedatives that Ruth kept giving me and the dreamlike swiftness of the next few days, I was already beginning to wonder if what had happened on Fortune Island had actually happened. When I asked Ruth about it, on those first days at the Brookline estate, all she would say is, "You've had a terrible nightmare, but you're coming out of it." Those words were comforting to hear, even if I didn't quite believe them, and they helped me to remove myself from what I knew to be true. "But Tom—"

"Tom is doing what he believes is right. If I didn't believe he was right, I wouldn't let him do it. I love Tom *because* he wants to do this, because he's the kind of man who would do this. This is his desire, his will, his wish—we have to respect him in this; our respect for what he's chosen to do is our love in action. Now go back to sleep and try to have a sweet dream. Believe me, there is no girl in the world loved more than you."

September on Fortune Island was not an autumnal month, but September in Boston can be nearly winter. The shock of the climatic change marked a change of life. Brookline is a suburb of Boston, so close, so integrated with the city that it might as well be Boston, and that September passed in a flash of adjustment from the tropical to the northern world, and the first snow filled the streets late in November. If sand dunes were white, it would look like that. Down and down the snow came with a raw wind. About a month after our arrival in Boston, Ruth discovered that she was pregnant with you, David. Had our dad known that you were on the way, would he have done what he did? Ruth made no attempt to tell him. The knowledge that you existed would probably have caused him to feel that his hope for redemption had been negated, that he had left stranded yet another hostage to fortune.

The Carolina newspapers gave us the bare outline of what he had done after we had left. He had brought Mrs. Walkup to the house and showed her the body. She had made contact with the authorities. He had told them that he had shot the Traveller for his own reasons, reasons that were none of their business. He had refused to cooperate with the court-appointed attorney, indeed, had refused to say anything except that he had shot the Traveller, had rejected a jury in favor of a judge, had pleaded guilty and was sentenced to twenty years in prison, back behind the Wall through the gates of which he had so shortly before emerged.

It appeared that he had placed the last brick in that wall without regret. Ruth's letters were returned unopened. But about six months later we received a letter from a priest who had apparently befriended him—a priest, and Tom was not a Catholic. Ruth said that he had probably chosen to talk to a priest because anything that slipped from him should not slip from the priest. Ruth believed that he'd needed someone to talk to, but even so wanted to keep his privacy. The priest wrote that he had written down the return address on the letters his friend Tom had rejected, feeling that he might need to tell someone someday of Tom's fate. It was a bad fate. There had been a riot in the prison, and Tom died, beaten to death, trying to protect a guard.

"He was a Christ-like man," the priest had written, and I remembered *The Imitation of Christ*, which I still thumbed through although I didn't consider myself a Christian anymore than Ruth considered herself a Jew. We had lost whatever it took. Tom Judas was no more. You, Ruth and I were what was left of him, and so we had a duty to him to do our best as he had done his best, mistaken as it might seem to others.

Biology became my subject and I tried to find in it, from the lowliest one-celled creatures to humans, how love progressed. I have been unsuccessful. But that it did progress into power, that it progressed to the point that it defied even the instinct of self-preservation, I have ample evidence. I *am* evidence. I have ample evidence in our dad, David, Tom Judas, that strange mysterious man who sought nothing for himself in life but that rarity, redemption.

V.

The dying woman could not go on reliving those last, horrifying events and the manuscript ends with her final attempt to rationalize them. In other words, Ruthie, Jessie gave up. Judging from a few extraneous scraps tucked in among the pages of the memoir, Jessie had plans to go further and round it out. In her stead, I'm going to try to do that.

My first thought is that the fact that she assumed and kept the name Judas until the end, indicates to me that she could never come to terms with the morality of the situation. I think she was plagued by guilt all her days, probably more so as she grew older and was able to gain perspective on the situation left behind at Fortune Island. For some people, good people, guilt can be a poison in their bloodstreams, and I can't help but think that bearing such guilt all her days must have shortened them, perhaps harmed her immune system and left her open to the cancer that consumed her. But I'm not a doctor or a scientist, and this is only a fancy of mine, I suppose. And yet my instinct tells me that it is possible.

I buck at the thought that a person, even a young person, should go scott-free after killing someone, even if that person deserved killing. What will the new age think, the age of your future? Will it hold a more liberal view? I wish I could come back some day and ask you what you've made of this story. Were they right in doing what they did? Perhaps, Ruthie, you can come to terms with it in the pragmatic morality of some future time. I am left disturbed but sympathetic.

The alternative scenario would have left me with a father—but that's a selfish point of view. And what would have happened to Jessie? Perhaps, with the right lawyer, some claim could have been made for self-defense; but since she left the house, went some distance, found a pistol, and brought it back apparently for the purpose of killing the Traveller—well, that looks pretty premeditated. Of course she may have been in the disassociative state that she describes and perhaps could have been found not guilty for reasons of temporary insanity. There is certainly ample evidence that she wasn't in her right mind. But neither my father nor my mother were willing to risk it. It was my dad's desire above all things to protect Jessie, and he both failed and succeeded. He certainly failed in that he put the pistol within her reach, but how could he ever have dreamed that she would use it as she did. It wasn't even that kind of pistol, scarcely more than a target practice pop-gun. Deadly enough, however. Both he and my mother failed in not getting Jessie away from the Traveller in time. They should have seen trouble coming. Perhaps they had become too involved with each other, too distracted. Perhaps it was the guilt over their involvement that led them to such a desperate act.

They did, however, ultimately succeed in giving her a life undarkened by public censure, but they lost each other in doing it, and my father lost me. Would he have done it, had he and mother been aware of my existence? Perhaps not, as Jessie suggested. But the more I think about the situation, the more the questions ramify. You'll have to answer them in your own way as they did in theirs and as I must seek to do in mine. But, Ruthie, I can't find it in my heart to disapprove of them in the final analysis. They were living the situation, as soldiers live war, and we are placed in the luxurious position of historians. We are given time to think, they had none. They had to act.

Of course I always knew what an extraordinary woman my sister was, but it took this little memoir of hers to make me realize just how extraordinary, and indeed, how extraordinary my mother was.

But Jessie, a lonely little girl on a nearly deserted island, growing without benefit of grade or high school, without even a friend with whom to talk, visited constantly by a monster, and yet becoming what she became, that *is* extraordinary!

I realize now that when we look at someone standing at a podium, receiving an award, an honor of some kind, or we see a picture of them in the paper holding a trophy, we rarely wonder what went into that life, what's behind the public view. Rarely, however, is there rape and murder behind that face, rarely in those eyes such terrible knowledge. But Jessie was too polite not to smile on the night of her triumph, and still her eyes, I see now, shuffling through the photographs of the event, as I couldn't see then, were haunted, as indeed were my mother's, and, I remember, for an instant, she and Jessie looked out over the audience, at me, looked for Tom, I am certain, or saw him in me as they chose to, and exchanged a look of the sort that had become a language between them, a language I had never learned to speak.

After the ceremony—I remember this vividly—my mother grabbed Jessie's arm, kissed her, and the two women walked off, half-supporting each other. Jessie was wrong about one thing, though. She needn't have hoped for forgiveness from me—none was required. I know that they all did their best back in a time and in a place and in circumstances of which they were so kind as to keep me blissfully unaware.

PART II.

THE FINAL TITHE

It was tax time, and the collectors had to deal with the usual greed—those who would hide what they still possessed behind tricks. A one-legged man danced up to a collector on two legs, in fear that if the collector knew that he had only one leg left he would have to surrender that. He had stuffed the false leg with bloody ground meat in an attempt at deception. The collectors laughed at this clumsy attempt at fraud and fined the man his left ear. All along the avenue the queue of cripples stretched and into the distance and on out of sight; for the State, having taken all else of value from the masses, had been reduced to taking cuts of meat from their bodies. Sometimes an eye was popped, sometimes a hand was cut off, depending entirely upon the taxpayer's indebtedness to the government. Sometimes so little was left of a taxpayer that he or she was brought forward on a stretcher, a mere skeleton with no more than a tenth of a life left, like a final tithe. In such case, the skin was stripped and the bones collected, resulting, finally, in death. The collectors were disgusted with the greed of these people, who showed signs of rational self-interest, rather than the altruism taught in the State schools. Without the flesh of the masses, it was wondered, how could the elite meet to eat? It was an eternal question, but above their pay scale, and they tried not to think of what would happen when no one was left but the elite themselves.

A MAN OF CONSCIENCE

The night can sweat with terror as before
We pieced our thoughts into philosophy,
And planned to bring the world under a rule,
Who are but weasels fighting in a hole.
—W.B. Yeats

This happened in London, although it could have happened in Dublin or New York or any major city of the world. It could have happened in some backwater as well, but it happened in London, not far from Piccadilly Circus. But where it happened is of no real importance—when is more relevant, but that will become clear in the telling of it. The story derives from a Scotland Yard confession, to which the author was privy before his retirement.

It was early evening of a cold November day. The pavements glistened under falling heavy mist and traffic sounds were muted. Two men were walking down a street. The man following came up behind the man ahead. The man ahead felt the barrel of a pistol in his back. He was told to keep walking and was ordered into a dark doorway.

"This was a trick," he said in a hushed voice, back over his shoulder. "I was told this was a meet for the cause."

"Get down those stairs."

The man ahead did as he was told and at the bottom was pushed through a door. Inside, the room was dark but the man behind switched on a light. It was a dank basement room of ancient drooling bricks, criss-crossing pipes, dust and cobwebs, deep below the street. There was a table. A few chairs. An old desk. Little else except looming shadows. The man ahead saw a rat stand up and look at him in a far corner when the light went on. Then he was struck a stunning blow to the back of his head. He couldn't think. He fell to the cement floor and as he fell the Uzi he kept in an inside pocket of his trench-coat was ripped away. Minutes passed. Then consciousness returned.

"Awake?" said the man with the guns. He held the Uzi in his left hand and a long-barrelled Webley in his right.

"Yes." The man on the floor looked around. As he took in this filthy empty room he was filled with fear and at the same time outrage.

"Where am I?" Then he realized that he was bound hand and foot with duct tape, could not move. "Where am I? Who are you? What's this? Who are you? What *is* this?" His head was clearing. "Obviously, you are not the man I was supposed to meet."

"I am the man you were supposed to meet—inevitably. I'm your punisher. No, your redeemer. We are Napoleon and Wellington at Waterloo."

"Punisher? My what? Is that what you said?" Then he felt outrage become rage and raw anger. "Who in hell are you? Some kind of maniac?"

"Of course, we are both maniacs, living in a mad insane-simian world. I told you, I'm your punisher."

"My punisher . . ." he muttered to himself, "my punisher." Then, he looked up intently and saw, for the first time, a tall thin man with a salt-and-pepper mustache, a sharp pointed aquiline nose and eyes pale as ice-water. The man's demeanor portrayed no emotion, only purpose. Now the bound man felt a thrill of uncontrollable fear as he looked at the neat gray overcoat and the gray fedora downward slanted over the cold pale eyes.

"My punisher? For what? And who in hell are you to punish me? Some kind of damn fascist cop? Where is this place? How did I get here? Oh, yeah, I remember. You stuck a gun in my back. Why did you have to hit me so hard? My brain's scrambled."

"Better now?"

"I can see straight, but you've given me a thudding headache. What's this all about? I can see your intention isn't robbery, so what is it?"

"As to where you are, this is Purgatory. You are on your way to hell."

"What then, are you some damn loony representative of the Church? An agent for the Vatican or something? I don't have to tell you, do I, that I don't believe in hell?"

The tall thin man spoke slowly, with supreme confidence, "Oh, oh, I assure you, you're going to hell, whether you believe in it or not."

"You know it, then?"

"It? What?"

"Hell."

"I'm a veteran of several wars as are you. I've had your file for some time. You've sunk from soldier to terrorist."

"Hell—ha! Now look you, enough of these crazy metaphysics. Who are you and—"

"I'm not being metaphysical. Quite the contrary."

"What are you talking about?"

"I mean that I've been thinking about you for a long time. And I guess there's a hell. If you exist, there must be a hell to swallow you up. Maybe not in the earth, but on the surface of it. And that's where you're going."

The bound man thought that perhaps he was dealing with a real lunatic. This was no ordinary stick-up or assault or kidnapping that one in his business might expect. He thought he'd better go easy here. He felt that he was dealing with a fanatic. "Now look," he said, "just explain to me why you have me tied up in this room? Tell me who you are. Explain!"

Dreamlike, the tall thin man said: "Who you are. Who I am . . ."

"Damn maniac!"

"Yes. I used to think you were the maniac. Maybe you are. But it won't change anything. I'm—" he searched for the right word— "implacable. But I know who you are. You, in particular. But I know who you all are."

The bound man struggled in the tape and tried to sit up straight. "All right. I think I've got it now. Oh, damn, I've got a headache. Damn, my head aches! You must be some kind of agent . . . CIA, FBI, MI5—something. This is an interrogation. Want information? Is that it?"

"No."

"No? Look, maybe I can help you. Give you some information. I know plenty. What is it you want?"

"At first I thought I wanted you dead. But as I thought about it I realized that would be no punishment for you. It would only set you free."

The bound man felt apprehensive. He couldn't figure this guy out. "Revenge?"

"I suppose so. But the more I thought about that the less important it seemed. Anyway, revenge must be taken in hot blood. There's satisfaction in that. There's no satisfaction in what I'm going to do. Indeed, I've condemned myself to a life of misery. You've brought me to this."

"Not revenge? Not revenge! What then? What are you going on about? What do you mean, condemn yourself to a life of misery? Why?"

"I'm a man of conscience."

"Conscience?" The bound man thought as fast as he could and said, "Look, are you some kind of madman, or what? Is there any water here? Got any aspirin? I feel nauseated. How long was I out?"

"Ah. I wonder."

"Now what's that supposed to mean?"

"I've been thinking about you for a long time. About this day. Suppose we say . . . suppose we say that I'm the husband of a secretary whose hands were blown off, opening one of your letter bombs."

"Are you?"

The tall thin man put his revolver on the table, fished in the desk drawer and brought out a bottle of brandy, a tin of aspirin, two glasses. "No," he said, as he stepped back and leaned down to the bound man. "Open your mouth. And yes." He took out a few aspirin and put two on the bound man's tongue, then poured brandy to wash them down.

"Now what's that supposed to mean?"

"It means that it might be the case, but it's no longer the major reason. It means, as I said before, vengeance must be taken in hot blood. I am not your punisher. I am your redeemer." He became more excited as he spoke, his voice trembled and rose in heat and volume. The single overhead light made the creases in his face seem to jump and rearrange themselves as he paced back and forth in front of the bound man. "It means that right after your plastique blew my old father to pieces in Dublin I wanted to kill you. In hot blood! I wanted revenge. Vengeance! Who wouldn't? But I cooled off. It means that after my friend Izak, the great Olympic runner, had his legs severed by a blast of machine gun fire in an airport. . . . It means that I wanted revenge for Izak! It means that I wanted to kill you. In hot blood! But I cooled off. It means that after my thirty daughters ranging in age from nine to ninety were blown up in a hotel ballroom in Paris—I wanted to kill you! In hot blood! It means that after eighteen Christmas holiday travellers in Vienna and Rome were blown apart at the airports, I wanted to kill you. But I cooled off. I cooled off."

"I don't know what you're talking about. I had nothing to do with Rome, Vienna, Paris. Thirty daughters in Paris?—you're completely mad!"

"Am I? Have I become mad? Might be." The self-called Redeemer shook his head as his voice lowered. "Ask any psychiatrist, madness is contagious. If I'm mad it's because you're mad. If I'm sane, you're sane, too. If we're both sane then there must be evil. If there is evil, there must be good. I've thought of all this. Finally, I don't know what to make of it, but that neither one of us is a civilized human being. And if human beings can be civilized, how does one account for endless wars? Isn't the human race a bunch of monkeys fighting over banannas and nuts? And I'm not a philosopher, I'm a . . . "

"Go on, what? What are you?"

"Can't make any difference, really. I've been a soldier."

"Ahhh. Now we're getting somewhere."

"Oh, well, we're not really getting to anything in the sense that you mean. Who hasn't been a soldier? A political killer? In a world where *you* exist, everyone's a soldier."

"What do you mean, *my* world?"

"As I said before, I'm a man of conscience."

"Couldn't you loosen this?" he asked, holding up his bound wrists. "I haven't got any circulation. My legs are asleep. You're not a torturer are you? You seem civilized."

"Seem civilized. *You* seem civilized—whatever that can mean. But it's a good question. I think the answer is that I'm about to become a deep torturer."

"Then why did you give me the aspirin and the drink? That's not the sort of thing a torturer does. That's the act of a humanist."

"Oh. . . I wanted your full attention. You can't pay any attention to me when you're suffering."

The bound man shook his head. "I don't understand you, I admit it. Deep torturer. What does that mean?"

"It means redeemer. It means I'm not out to punish your body."

"Then loosen these bonds."

"Perhaps. Even at this moment, I'm not certain which of us is mad."

"What do you mean, deep torturer?

"Redeemer. Redeemer! It means that I've thought and thought about it. I mean . . . look at the weapons you choose. The weapons of a terrorist, bombs and sprayed bullets. You are a terrorist. You are my terrorist and I am going to redeem you." He picked up the bound man's machine pistol from where he had put it on the table and waved it back and forth with contempt.

"My Uzi?"

"Yes. Look at it. Sprays venom. Now look at this." He takes his long barelled Webley revolver from the table, aims at the terrorist's head. "One shot." He cocks the revolver. "I am accurate. If I kill someone, it is my intention. I am not careless about murder."

"You don't mean to kill me, or you would have done it by now."

"I could hit you between the eyes at the distance of a city block."

"Meaning?"

"Meaning that I don't spray venom like a spitting reptile." He spat on the Terrorist's machine pistol and threw it into the dark corner where the rat had stood at attention. “Meaning that I’m selective. I choose my victim.”

“You sonofabitch!”

“Pointing my pistol at you was a wanton act. It was almost an act of torture. You see, I can tell the difference. I’ve still got enough humanity to possess a conscience. I know that what I just did was wrong, pointing my pistol at your head, cocking it. Oh, I’ve thought about it for a long time. No, I’m just a simple soldier. At first it was vengeance. But I cooled off. I thought about it. I asked myself what kind of human being . . . no, subhuman . . . could send letter bombs through the mail to blow off the hands of secretaries. I have access to files. I know your ilk. I know you, particularly. You’re . . . your family’s quite wealthy. You, dear boy, are a spoiled brat!”

“I have a cause!”

“You have a vanity!” the self-called Redeemer shouted. “You have an arrogance. You have a will to be constrained by no political system, nor any conscience. A terrorist kills to feel infantile power. If you got what you want, it would pall immediately. Immediately you’d want something else. Then and there. What you want is . . . is . . . obedience! Power over people. You are a great ape in a jungle. You are what civilization was meant to conquer.”

“I want to help in the struggle against fascism!”

“But, my boy, you *are* a fascist. Your life is telling other people what to do. It’s a disease in an adult, a mental illness. You see, every baby is born a fascist. Every baby wants what it wants when it wants it. And this is as it should be. And every baby will use every means at its disposal to get what it wants. And what parent, late at night, has not been the victim of a torturing baby, who uses its shrill cry to make you move and move quick. Babies are fascists—one in the same. And you, my boy, have simply never grown up. You see, you're that thing most to be feared . . . a willful child with a machine gun or bomb." He walked over to the dark corner and picked up the machine pistol, came back and held it under the terrorist's nose, pushed it into his face.

You see?" He went back to the table and dropped it there, picked up his Webley and said, "A man's weapon. The weapon of a skillful, selective, mature human being."

"You're as crazy as they come."

"Admittedly. As I told you, I'm not a philosopher. I'm a soldier."

"Not a torturer, or so you say. Loosen these tapes."

"Why not? The Redeemer took out a switchblade, snapped it open and cut the Terrorist free.

"Oh, God, I'm like putty," the Terrorist said, rubbing his arms and legs to get the circulation going. He tried to stand but his knees would not cooperate.

"Oh, you're a helpless victim. How does it feel?"

"Not so helpless in a few minutes. Let me get my blood flowing."

"The thing is, you're like an infant. During the course of growing up, you never acquired a conscience. No, you've been deprived. When you commit an act of terrorism, apparently it doesn't trouble you that you've made handless or legless or sightless, or lifeless, another human being."

"What about you? You're a bloody soldier. You've wounded people. Killed them."

"Yes. Troublesome, isn't it? I've thought about it. As I was preparing for this I thought a good deal about it. The only thing I can come up with is the fact of randomness."

"What about your bloody bombs? What about Dresden? Hiroshima? Nagasaki? London? Bunch of sonofabitching soldiers doing that, wasn't it? There were innocents in those cities, weren't there?"

"Oh, God!"

"Don't call Him in on it now."

"Yes. That's a terrible question."

"Nothing selective there, eh?"

"Yes, it amounts to the question—don't you think—of whether we're all mad or sane, and, therefore, evil, and that, then, there must be good, too. Doesn't it amount to that?"

"Look, you bastard, I'm no bloody philosopher, either."

The Redeemer saw that fear had receded from his victim's eyes. "Crawl back, over there," he said, indicating direction away from himself. The Terrorist saw resignation in the pale eyes of his captor, some kind of loss, and sadness.

"Stay on the floor. Back! Maybe the answer is that evil is who initiates . . . who starts the thing."

"To hear you talk, babies start it."

"It's that we're wild animals, not yet fully human. No, I've got to stay with my point. My only sanity is my point."

"Which is?"

"That people have to suffer for the crimes they commit. . . for the evil they do. That they can't suffer unless they have a conscience, and they can't develop a conscience without suffering. That that's what I mean by deep torture. I think the difference between you and me is that I have a conscience. It does seem different to me—that if a man tries to kill me, in defending myself, I kill him—than if I were the one who decided to do the killing first. That does seem different to me. The secretary didn't try to kill you."

"I didn't try to kill her, either. I didn't know she existed." The Terrorist was exasperated. With the impetus his freed limbs gave him he grabbed one of the chairs and sat, while the Redeemer followed his movements with his gun.

"You didn't care," said the Redeemer. "You haven't got the imagination, the empathy required. No, you see, there's the point. You just meant to inflict pain, death, upon someone, anyone. That's your power. Yes. Yes. That's the point. You were the initiator."

"So I'm the bloke without a conscience, is that it?"

"That's it."

"Your point! Your point! Oh, I get your point, all right. It doesn't make a hellova lot of sense. *My* point is that we're in a war here so—the war of the apes."

"But you are permanently out of the war. You may get your circulation back, but you are not going back into circulation. No, not you."

"You mean you're going to hold me prisoner? You said before that you didn't intend to kill me."

"I don't. That's why I'm going to have to be very careful."

"You do intend to torture me then?"

"I'm going to have to inflict pain. But I would do what I intend to do without inflicting pain if I could."

"Damn you! What is it you intend to do?" The Terrorist thought he could lunge for this lunatic. He waited for the right moment.

"When you leave here," said the Redeemer, "and you will leave, you will be a changed man. You will begin a lifelong process of learning remorse. I'm going to make you grow up, laddie buck. You're going to learn what it is really like to share this planet with other members of your species. In your mind, which will gradually develop a heart, a conscience, you will be deeply tortured for the rest of your life. Because you have never understood what it is to see yourself in another being—sympathy—empathy. You've been locked in a cell all your life, laddie. But I'm going to lock you in so tight and for so long that you'll scream night and day for the word of another human being. For the sight of a face. For the grace to move with another in a dance. Even now, I can hear your *cri de coeur*. It is sweet to my ears."

"What in hell are you going to do?"

"I'm going to lock you in your body. All by yourself."

"What? What? What?"

"I'm going to cut your tongue out, so that you'll never be able but to vomit sound. I'm going to hold this pistol next to your eardrums and fire it, so that you'll never hear the sound of a voice again. I'm going to use my thumbs on your eyes. I'm going to castrate you. And I'm going to break your elbows and knees, and I'm going to see to it that you live. And for the rest of your days your punishment will be . . . isolation."

"And you, you bastard, you call yourself a man of conscience?"

"Oh, I know, I know. I've thought about it a great deal. I've thought it all out for a long, long time."

"You can't do it! You haven't got it in you, to do a thing like that. You're just trying to frighten me."

"Yes. I can do it because I hate your kind beyond reason. But, at first, I thought I couldn't do it unless—"

"Unless?"

"Unless, after I'd done it, I killed myself."

"My God, you mean to do it, don't you?" The terrorist was dizzy with this talk. One minute he thought his captor a garden variety nut case whom he could overtake and the next, some horrible philosophical maniac whose black whirling nonsense was seeping into his own reasoning.

"Yes, I mean it. But then I thought. . . then I thought that would be cheating."

"Cheating what? God?"

"No. Myself. My conscience. You see, if I want you to suffer remorse, then I have no right to escape it. That's what I meant when I said earlier that in condemning you, in . . . acting as your therapist, in awarding you the gift of a conscience . . . well, how could I run out on my own?"

The Terrorist realized then that only one chance for him existed. He lunged at the Redeemer in desperation.

In a reflex action the Redeemer jerked the trigger of his cocked Webley and a red hole appeared between the Terrorist's unbelieving eyes.

"Oh no—Oh God!" the Redeemer cried, as the Terrorist fell to the floor. "O no, O *God*!"

Later, out of that place, in the icy splash of mist, still shaken, he walked the streets without purpose or direction, among average people who were just trying to live.

PART III.

SUBJECTS IN MIRROR

Not on its reflecting surface, but in the depths of the mirror, the "scenes" appeared. I turned away, then back, incredulous, aware of the tricks the mind can play. Friends, relatives, lovers, even barely-met workmen, the electrician who came to do some wiring, the plumber who came to fix the pipes, the cable man, the woman from the next apartment who had lost her keys, and some I did not remember or recognize, all stared into their own eyes, into their nostrils and mouths, picking and probing—even the baby-sitter with her young lover behind her, watching her own young lust, whom I thought to have been so innocent. And then there was somewhere else, a room not recognizable, a previous place, the mirror apparently having travelled, and a strange, beautiful woman, her long, fair, platinum-streaked hair unravelled to her narrow waist, over her bare bronzed shoulders and breasts; and oh that scene was worse than the earlier scenes, with those unabashed, secret performers, most of whom I thought I knew, for nothing moved but the woman's jade eyes, up and down, back and forth, even more lustful for herself than any man might show himself to be, had he been watching her. And I realized now how sickeningly full the mirror was, a mirror of disturbing and disgusting emotions; and, as I watched the self-love burning in the beautiful woman's eyes in the mirror that had given up its secrets, my throat ached and I began to choke with tears; and that was when the mirror broke, and I withdrew my bleeding hand, which had been reaching in to touch what was in the terrible, honest mirror.

MANSLAUGHTER

Mother me out of here.
—Theodore Roethke

I.

A disheveled Tod Mitchell sat at the head of his large dining room table, drinking beer from a glass mug. His mother, Spring, had arrived at her son's Brooklyn apartment a few minutes before, and had brought along her new boyfriend, "Butsy" Suddeth, a short, red-headed, handsome man some years her junior. Spring got up from the table, leaned down and then grabbed her son around the neck, kissed him on the cheek, and said breathlessly, "I still can't believe it! It's just wonderful!"

"I got up about nine with a terrific bloody hang-over," Tod said, "and I was just having a Heineken's—trying to get my head together—when the phone rang. Well, when I heard the voice the thought flashed through my mind: What's Jerry," he looked at "Butsy," explaining, "that's my agent, what's Jerry doing calling me on a Saturday morning? I was still in a fog. 'Well,' he says, 'I've sold your novel.' I didn't think I'd heard him right. He had to say it a few more times before I could take it in. He says: 'I've got you an advance of five grand'—which is really pretty good for a first novel—and I've got some film people interested.'" Tod looked at them. "That's a big deal!"

"I can't believe it," said Spring, sitting back down, shaking her head.

"But it's true, Mom. It's really true! I'm supposed to start work with an editor at Triumph next week. But there isn't a lot to do—just small changes."

"Well, you've worked hard enough for it, I must say. You deserve a lot of credit."

"I can't wait to tell Gracie. She'll faint, just watch and see."

"Where did you say she went?"

"To Macy's. She went up to do some shopping. I wish she'd call so I could tell her. She'll just faint when she hears." Tod turned to "Butsy."

"Want another drink, er . . . "

"Fred—Fred Suddeth, but everybody calls me 'Butsy' on account of I smoke cigars all the time. Boy, I really walked in on something, didn't I?"

"Looks like you did, Butsy—it's going to be a party all day—all night—all weekend, maybe!" said Tod. He got up from the table and went to the kitchenette for more drinks for the company and kept talking. "Bourbon or beer—or both? See, Mom was supposed to come over yesterday, er—Butsy—but she never shows up when she says she will. Hell, I got depressed waiting for her. I was supposed to be working—writing. But she said she'd be over, so I didn't work."

"I just didn't have the energy, Tod."

Butsy smiled, glancing at Spring and said, "I guess not." Then he looked at Tod and explained, "We went out dancing Thursday night, so on Friday we—" At that instant Spring kicked Butsy's shin under the table and gave him a "be quiet" look. She didn't want him saying too much about what they'd been doing.

Tod put a pitcher of beer and a bottle of bourbon on the table and said, "Well, that's O.K., but why didn't you call? I could have gone ahead with my work. I waited all day for you. It got me all off my schedule for nothing."

"I wasn't sure whether I'd come or not."

"Well . . . Well, never mind. It's a happy day. One of the best of my life."

"What's your book about?" Butsy said.

"It's about my mother and my father and me, growing up absurd. It's called *Walking the Edge.*"

"I don't know nothing about books. But I can tell you this—your Mom sure is a good dancer."

"I know. I don't think she's ever going to grow old—or up."

"I don't want to grow up," Spring said. "If you grow up you grow old and I don't have any intention of growing old." And, as if to add emphasis to her declaration, she said, "Let's put some music on, Tod."

"Anything to please," said Tod. He walked over to the record player in the bookcase, shuffled through a few albums and put on an old romantic Harry James. "Can you believe it?" he said quietly, almost to himself, "I'm a novelist!"

"And don't forget that five thousand dollars!" Spring called over to him, "But, you know, you don't seem all that excited about it."

"I'm still in shock, I guess."

Butsy was reminded of a time when he too, had been in shock. "I was in a movie once," he said.

Spring, whether she meant to contradict, or just add to Butsy's comment, said: "Butsy's' a jockey."

"*Used* to be a jockey," he said. "Mostly nowadays I just play the nags."

"Butsy's a sporting man," Spring said.

"Yeah, that's it. You got some Mom here, Tod, and a good little drinker."

"She's a sport, all right," Tod conceded.

"Oooh, all this attention!" Spring said. "I love it!"

"I met your Mom a few months ago, over in Jersey, at a bar—a nice place, you know—and she was behaving like a perfect lady. That's what I said to myself—that's a perfect lady."

Tod was amused by Butsy's impression of Spring and said, "Oh, she's not always such a perfect lady. Are you, Mom?"

"I hope not," she said, smiling.

Butsy didn't quite get the joke and said, "Hey, you shouldn't talk like that to your mother."

"Butsy's Irish," Spring said to Tod.

"She kids me about being holy. So O.K., that's the way I was brought up. Anyhow, she's Irish herself, ain't she? She told me that she wanted to be a nun when she was a little girl."

"She wasn't cut out for a nun," said Tod.

Spring stood up and downed her beer. "Let's drink to that!" she said. "Let's drink to that and then let's dance. Come on," she said, "I want to dance with my son, the author." She held out a hand to Tod. They were good dancers, but unyielding to each other's desire to lead. Butsy sat, amused, curious, humming, and puffing on his cigar as they stumbled about. As the dance ended, Butsy applauded and Tod bowed to his mother. He sat back down, wiped his brow, and drained his beer mug. Butsy got up and danced Spring about the parquet floor, occasionally puffing at his cigar. He danced in the style of an earlier era, doing deep dips, and whispering in Spring's ear. Tod watched until the dance ended, then went to the refrigerator in the little kitchenette and brought back more beer.

Butsy began to hum, and then to croon "The Christmas Song."

"Chestnuts roasting on an open fire . . . . That's one colored guy had a beautiful voice, that Nat Cole."

"You have a beautiful voice," Spring said. "Doesn't he, Tod? Butsy's a real crooner."

"I wish Gracie would call," said Tod, distracted. "What time is it, anyway?"

Butsy looked at his watch and said, "It's noon. Hey, what do you think of this watch? It's digital. How much do you think it cost?"

"I couldn't guess," said Tod.

"Nothing. It got stuck on my wrist." He laughed.

"Butsy! Listen, why don't you go and get us some food," Spring suggested. "If this is going to be a party, we need some cold cuts."

"Sure, is there a deli around here?"

"Straight down the hill, Butsy, two blocks," said Tod. "But I should do the buying. You're my guests. Trouble is, I haven't got any money." He laughed. "Flat broke."

"Tapped out?" Butsy asked.

"Tap city."

"Don't worry. Butsy'll buy," said Spring.

"Sure," Butsy said. "I hit it big at the track last week. I'll get some more beer, too. Back in a jiff." He got up, put on his jacket and went to the door, giving them a little wave as he closed it behind him.

Tod said to his mother, "Where did you find him?"

"Do you like him?" she asked.

"He's O.K." Tod said, and shrugged.

"Sort of common, eh?"

"I don't think of people that way, Mom. But he's a thief, isn't he?"

"Oh, he just picks things up. He does it more for the game. But he sure is a comedown from your father, isn't he?"

"I'll have to admit that."

"I miss your father so." Spring was silent for a few moments. "I was just thinking the other day—it'll soon be his birthday. He died five years ago. Where does the time go? You're so much like him, Tod."

"Not much, really. He was a gentleman."

"You're a gentleman."

"I can act like one when I have to. He didn't know how not to be one, anymore than he knew how to stay sober for thirty days in a row."

"I loved him but I never understood him. Tod, you don't mind me going out with men, do you?"

"Absolutely not, Mom. You've got a lot of living to do. I want you to do it."

"Then you didn't really mean what you said."

"What?"

"What you called me on the phone. A whore."

"Of course I didn't mean it. I'm Irish too, you know. But don't you remember what got me started?"

"I know."

"You didn't call me or let me know where you were for three months. I was going crazy with worry. I called the police. Missing persons. The hospitals. Everyone. The Fire Department! And all the time you were shacked up with some guy who told you that calling me meant that you loved me more than you did him. It's crazy. Naturally, when you finally did call and told me how things stood I was upset—angry—by God, I was furious! What did you expect? There you are, sixty-six years old, and vanished somewhere in the wilds of New Jersey—"

"Sixty-four!"

"O.K., *sixteen*! My sixteen-year-old mother vanishes one day, only to turn up three months later, to say that her boy-friend—of whom I've never heard—told her not to call me. A stranger to both of us!"

"I know. I was wrong. I just didn't want to cause any trouble."

"Cause any trouble! Think of the distraction! I couldn't write! How do you think I felt? Are you trying to kill me?"

"Well, let's get off that now."

"Why? Just because you want to? It always has to be your way, doesn't it? To hell with me!" Tod sat silent, staring into his beer mug. It was an old argument.

"Tod, let's not fight. This is a big day. You've sold your novel. Think of it! My son, the novelist!"

"And here I was, pretty newly married, and I couldn't even invite my mother for a visit because I didn't know where she was. It played havoc with my nerves."

"You're not the only one with nerves."

"And I think Gracie lost the baby because of what happened."

"She lost the baby because of Billy Shaw and all that upset. And that happened because of your drinking."

"Well, who taught me to drink? It's the only thing I ever saw as a kid. You and Dad! Parties and dead soldiers!"

"Other people survive their parents without becoming drunks."

"Yeah, if they've got something else. What the hell did I have? I never went to school. No brothers or sisters—thanks to your abortions—or even any friends. I was just locked up alone with you two and your drinking. Kept with you so you wouldn't have to worry about me. Not even let out of those dismal apartments to play on the street. I played under the table with your feet kicking at me. At least you could have sent me off to school in the morning."

"You know we moved too often for you to go, to keep regular. We were in and out of town in a week."

"There *were* laws."

"Oh, we did get into trouble. Do you remember the time when the truant officer came to our door to check on you, and Dad was standing across the street—" She smiled at Tod.

Yes, Tod remembered, of course he remembered. It was a funny memory they shared. "Dad just left the house, going somewhere—" he said.

"He was going off to his territory to sell," Spring

said. "And when he saw this nice-looking man at our door—"

Tod laughed. "He came charging back, thinking the man was your secret lover—"

"And you should have seen the look on his face when I introduced them. 'This is Mr. Whoever-it-was, the truant officer—'"

They both laughed and laughed until they were interrupted by the ringing of the telephone. Tod jumped up and ran to the phone. "That must be Gracie." He looked back at Spring and shook his head, no.

"Hello," he said. "No, I thought it was Gracie. Yeah. She's gone shopping. Macy's, Manhattan, I think. You're home early. Half day, today? Yes, sure, come on down. We're having a party. Yes. I have some wonderful news. Wait till you hear, Jean. O.K., 'bye."

"What's she doing home at this hour?" Spring said. "I thought she did some kind of counseling or something on Saturdays."

"She does. But it was a half day today."

"Is she getting adjusted to being a widow?"

"I suppose so. She seems all right."

"It's easier at her age. She's young."

"I don't know. Being a widow at twenty-five must be different from being one at sixty-five but who can say that it's easier?"

"That's probably right. You're very wise for such a young man."

"I'm not such a young man and I'm smart enough, at least, to know that I'm not very wise."

"There you go, always taking exception to everything I say. Isn't there anything about your old mother that you like?"

"Why, I like everything about my not-so-old mother," he said, and gave her a hug.

There was a knock at the door and Tod went to answer it. He held the knob, turned back to her and said, "Except that she tells me one thing and does another. She tells me she'll be over on Friday and makes me give up a day's work—which makes me get drunk, which gives me a hangover—and then she shows up on Saturday with a stranger in tow." He turned away from her and opened the door to a pretty, young brunette.

Jean Shaw was an upstairs neighbor. She stepped into the room with familiarity and said, "Hi, Tod. Oh, hello, Mrs. Mitchell. I didn't know you were visiting. How are you?"

"Jean, you know I like you to call me Spring. I'm fine. How're you?" Spring got up and gave the young woman a hug.

"I'm lucky today. I got off early."

Spring sat back down at the table. "I don't know how you can stand it, being with children all week and then again on Saturday," she said. "I know I couldn't bear it. I remember—"

Tod recognized the direction of his mother's often-repeated story, and changed the trajectory: "Sit down, Jean. Want a drink? A beer?"

"Sounds good."

Spring took up the thread of her story, "Well, I had six little sisters and brothers and one older sister who refused to do a thing. We were very poor. Our father had died at only twenty-nine—and Mama worked as a cook in a girls' school and was away most of the time and it fell to me to take care of all those kids—and I used to say to myself: Spring, I'd say, when you grow up don't you ever be such a fool as to get married and have children. I even thought I might become a nun."

"But you didn't. You got married and had me." Tod lifted his mug to Jean, smiled at her and tilted his head toward his mother with an expression of 'here we go again' on his face.

"Well, yes. I fell in love with your father. That's what kind of fool I am, as the song says."

"Thanks a lot."

"Well, I didn't mean—"

"Of course not," said Tod. "How do you think it makes me feel every time you say that? I've heard it all my life."

"You know I don't mean . . . That's just the way I chatter on. I don't mean anything."

"You don't think about the way you make other people feel."

"Oh, let's get off me. Tell Jean the news."

"Yes, what is it, Tod?"

"Tod sold his book," said Spring.

"Oh, Tod! How wonderful! Have you told Gracie? What did she do?"

"She doesn't know yet," Tod said.

"No," said Spring. "She's been out all day."

"Oh, I've got to stay and see her reaction. I know she'll be in her glory. She always believed in you and she loved that book. So did I. And so did Billy. We knew how good it was."

"So did I," said Spring.

"You!" Tod knew that she'd never read a word he'd written.

"Well I did. Of course I did."

"I don't know how you could have. After depriving me of any education whatsoever, you told me I couldn't be a writer because I didn't have any education."

"Well, I didn't know anything about those things. I had to leave school in the sixth grade to go to work in a mill. You should have asked your father. He was the big brain. He went to college."

"Yeah, Dreiser's mother didn't know anything about those things either. He had to teach her to read. But she said that he could be or do anything he wanted to be or do. She didn't constantly put him down in order to exalt her own feeble ego. Vanity! All is vanity!"

Spring turned to Jean and said, jokingly, "Let's ignore him. He's drunk."

"Let's do. Until he cheers up."

There was a knock at the door and Spring got up to answer. "That must be Butsy," she said. Butsy came in, an enormous load of groceries in his arms. There was a young delivery boy behind him, pushing a loaded shopping cart.

"What's all this?" Spring said. "Where have you been so long?"

"What's it look like? I've been shopping," he said, leading the boy. "Come on in, kid. Push it in here."

Spring said, "My God, what did you get?"

"I got some of everything. I mean, this is a party, ain't it?" Tod helped Butsy and Spring unload the cart and passed a few cans to Jean.

“Stuffed artichoke hearts!” said Spring. “Canned lobster! Crabmeat!”

“How did they get in there?” said Butsy. “ I don’t remember payin’ for them.”

“Butsy, you didn’t!”

Oblivious, Butsy turned to the delivery boy. “Here kid, buy yourself a chocolate cigar,” he said. The delivery boy thanked him and left, pushing the cart ahead.

Butsy called after him, “More where that came from, kid.”

“Sure I did, Spring. I got plenty to spend—easy come, easy go—and I don’t mind spendin’ it; but those supermarkets are a bunch of crooks. You think I should pay for lobster at their prices when the lobsters are running all over the ocean? Look!” He took two small glass jars from his pockets and said, “Butsy’s got the magic touch.”

To Tod and Jean, Spring said, “Butsy’s got light fingers.” Then, to Butsy she said, “What do you think Tod and Jean must think of you?”

Tod said, “I’m with Butsy. The supermarkets are a bunch of crooks. They take us, we should take them. More power to you, Butsy!”

“Me too,” Jean joined in.

“There, you see?” said Butsy. “They think I did right.”

“But suppose you got caught?” said Spring.

“Hell, I been lifting stuff all my life and never got caught yet.”

“There’s always a first time,” said Spring.

“They only warn you the first time. Gimme a drink, will you, somebody? That hill’s a hot climb.”

Tod led Butsy to a chair, got him a fresh beer and said, "Butsy, this is a friend of ours—Jean Shaw. She lives upstairs. Jean, Fred Suddeth, a friend of Mom's."

"Nice meetin' ya," he said.

"Same here—er . . . . "

From over in the kitchenette, still putting away groceries, Spring called, "Call him Butsy."

"Yeah—call me Butsy. Everybody does."

"That's an unusual name."

"Because—see—" He fished in his breast pocket, found a half-smoked cigar, and began to light it.

"Ah! And what do you do, Butsy?"

Spring called again from the kitchenette, "Butsy's a jockey."

"*Was* a jockey. Now I'm a sporting man. Anybody can see I'm too old to be a jockey—and too fat. She's always building me up to her friends. What do you think? Something wrong with what I am?"

"Not that I can see," said Jean.

"Hey, I like this one. You I like. Good-lookin' too."

Spring came to the table and said, kiddingly, "Watch out there." Whether she meant it for Butsy or Jean, was unclear.

"You better watch out, Spring. Butsy is very handsome—in a rugged, red-headed way. My husband, Billy, was a red-head."

"That right? Oh, I'm old enough to be your father."

"*Grand*father, you mean." said Spring.

"I wouldn't say that." He leaned over toward Jean and said, "She's always tearing me down."

"I thought she was always building you up."

Butsy said to her, "Well, like this, see: building up what I do, tearing down what I am."

Tod plopped down beside Butsy and nursed his beer. He looked distant and rather gloomy. He said, "I know the feeling."

Jean looked at Butsy and said, "What *do y*ou do, Butsy? What's a sporting man, anyway?"

Tod said, "Butsy's a gambler, I think."

"Spring, you got a sharp son here."

"Nothing sharp about it. You said you were flush from the track."

"Did I? I get a few drinks, I forget."

"Butsy, did you stop off along the way? I think you stopped off and had a few somewhere. All that shopping should have cleared your head."

"Well, I hadda, Christsake! Oops! Shouldn't take the name of the Lord thy God in vain. I mean, here I am all of a sudden sitting around with a guy who writes books—me, who on'y reads the headlines and funnies and sports pages of the Daily News. I'm nervous."

"You? Nervous?" Spring said.

"Yeah—me—nervous! I'm human, you know." Butsy looked over at Tod and said, "All the way over here from Jersey I'm thinking: I got to behave very elegant now because I'm meetin' Spring's son who is a writer. And I got nervous."

"You're not nervous now, are you?"

"Nah. Not so much now. First thing I see you drinking beer I say to myself: This is a regular guy."

"I told you my son was no snob."

"But *you* are." Tod was clearly feeling his drinks. Numerous old battles with his mother were being reviewed in his mind.

"Aw, no," Butsy said, "don't talk unpleasant to your Mom. Look, Tod: I know I ain't got no education; but that don't mean I haven't learned something. And one thing I know is: a mother is the most wonderful thing in the world."

"Bravo!" Spring applauded. "I told you he was an Irishman."

"Hey, look at the Irish mug on her! I'm nuts about your Mom, Tod. She's what I call a lady."

"Well, thank you," Spring said, smiling.

"And you too—" Butsy said, looking over at Jean, "what'd you say your name was?"

"Jean."

"That's a pretty name. Hey, seems to me like I heard your husband was dead. Did I get that right?"

"Yes, he's dead."

"I was with him," Tod said. "It was an accident."

"Yeah? What kind of an accident? Oh, listen, I don't mean to make you talk about it if—"

"No, it's all right," said Jean. "I've got to get used to it."

Tod said, "We were out drinking together. Billy was my best friend. We'd been drinking all day . . . I tried to get him to come home but he didn't want to quit. Finally, I got him into a subway station, but he darted for a car and the doors closed behind him before I could get on. Next morning he was found dead at Coney Island. He'd apparently fallen down a flight of iron stairs from the elevated."

Tod looked at Jean, sorry for a moment that he'd told the story. He said, "Jean, are you—"

"No, I'm all right. That's what happened." She looked down into her beer glass, then, looking up, she said, "He had red hair, too, like yours, Butsy."

"Mine is all full of grey."

"He was a musician," Tod said.

"A classical musician," Spring added.

Butsy said, "Classical. Gee, I'm sorry."

"Come on, let's cheer up," Jean said, pushing her chair back from the table.

"I've got an idea," said Spring.

"What?"

"Let's surprise Gracie," she said. "We can get the place all spruced up—"

"A real party!" said Tod. "And thanks to Butsy we've got everything we need."

"We should decorate the place," said Jean.

"Yeah, like Christmas!" Butsy joined in.

"That's it," said Jean. "We'll get out all the Christmas decorations—chains and lights and everything and really make it look like a real party. Then when Gracie walks in we'll all jump up and shout: Surprise! Surprise! Hip, Hip, Hooray! Tod's book's been sold!" She jumped up and down, caught in excitement and flushed. As she calmed down she said to Tod, "Ah, Billy would have loved this so much. He thought you were a fine writer, Tod. He really loved that book."

Tod looked at her. Jean grabbed his hand and said, "Oh, this is a great idea. Come on, let's get started."

"I'll do the dirty dishes and clean up," said Spring, "and you start hanging the decorations. Don't forget the lights! I love bright, pretty lights!"

"What should I do?" said Tod.

"Nothing," Jean said. "What do you think the party's about? You're the one who wrote the book. You and Gracie. You can watch and supervise."

"I'd never have done it," Tod said, "if it hadn't been for her, you know."

"She always believed in you," Spring said.

"She must be a great gal," said Butsy. "Hey, what should I do?"

"You keep Tod company," said Spring. "Show him some of your card tricks."

Tod said, "She's the only person who ever helped or encouraged me."

"Amazing Grace," said Spring. Tod thought he heard a tinge of sarcasm in her voice. "Let's get busy," she said, jumping up. She went back to the kitchenette and began cleaning out the sink, rattling silverware and pots.

Jean went out the door, saying, "I'm going upstairs to get our Christmas decorations. We've got everything. *I've* got everything."

Butsy pulled a deck of cards from an inside pocket, broke the seal, and methodically shuffled them while he puffed on his teeth-clenched cigar and watched Spring admiringly.

Tod sat at the table, and stared off in space.

Butsy sat opposite Tod, but ignored him. He was busy with his cards and watched Spring as she worked in the kitchenette. “Ain’t she something?” he said, lasciviously, perhaps to himself, perhaps to Tod, “Ain’t she something?”

After about ten minutes Jean came back into the apartment, carrying a large cardboard box of Christmas decorations. She put it down on the table and got to work decorating the room. She left the door ajar and in a moment, quietly, a stooped, gaunt, once-beautiful old woman slipped into the room. She leaned on her cane and asked, in a cultivated British accent, “What’s this? It isn’t Hogmanay yet, is it? I feel like Rip Van Winkle.”

Tod, snapped out of his momentary reverie, got up and shook the woman’s hand, putting an arm around her shoulders. “Sophia,” he said, “I’ve had wonderful news! My novel’s been accepted by Triumph.”

Sophia Bennett lived in the basement of the old brownstone apartment house and was a writer, herself; a poet, in fact, and was a good friend to the younger couple.

“Really?” she smiled.

“We’re going to have a party,” said Jean, coming over to greet Sophia. “Oh, you know Tod’s mother, Sophia. And this is Mister—”

“Butsy, just call me Butsy. Do you live here, too?”

Sophia looked across the room to Spring and nodded hello. “How do you do, Mister Butsy? Yes, downstairs.”

Spring answered Sophia, “Mister Suddeth. That’s his nickname—Butsy.”

Tod led Sophia to the table and helped her to a chair. She looked at Butsy and asked, “Suddeth? What an odd name! Is it English?”

"Well, Irish-American," said Butsy. "Are you English?"

"Welsh—so you see, you needn't be defensive," she said. "Jean's Irish too. We are all Celts here. Well, congratulations, Tod! How wonderful for you! Now tell me about it. I can imagine how happy Grace must be."

"She doesn't know yet. She went off to Macy's before I got the news."

"We're making a surprise party for her," said Jean.

"Would you like a drink, Sophia?" Spring said.

"Yes, a whiskey, if it's available, and soda—no ice—thank you, Spring. You must be very proud of Tod. This is certainly his red letter day."

Spring went off to the kitchenette to fix the drink, and called back, "I certainly am!"

"She was telling me all about him on the way over from Jersey," Butsy said. "I was sort of scared to meet a writer until she told me what a regular guy he was—how he was a shoeshine boy as a kid—like me—and had been in the Marines and all. She said how he never had no education to speak of, how he educated himself. We're from the school of hard knocks, ain't we, Tod?"

"But Tod is a very well educated man," said Sophia. "He went to New York University."

"On the G.I. Bill," said Tod.

Jean called down to Butsy from her perch on a chair where she was tacking up Christmas lights, "Sophia is a writer, too—a poet—"

"And," Tod said, "an actress. She once worked with Leslie Howard on the stage. Do you remember him?"

"That English actor who was with Bogart in 'Petrified Forest.' Sure, I know all Bogie's movies. I started to say before how I was in a movie. It was 'High Sierra,' where I did the fall for Bogart. You know. When he rolls down the mountain. That was me rolling."

"Really," Sophia said. "Were you a stuntman?"

Spring chimed in, "He's more of a story-teller. He's making that up."

"Well, I did do some stunt work. I told you. Before I was a jockey."

"That's very interesting," said Sophia. "What do you do now?"

"He's a sporting man," said Spring. She handed Sophia her drink and sat down with the others.

"I'm a gambler," he said.

"I like to gamble," Jean said.

"So do I," said Spring. "It's fun."

"Ah, Monte Carlo," Sophia said, with a flutter, kidding them a little, "when I was a young thing!"

"Not me," Tod said. "I want something I can count on."

"But Tod," said Sophia, "you've gambled all along. You've gambled on yourself, and your very life! And you've won!" The old woman was obviously very happy for her young neighbor. She had spent many evenings with Tod and his Grace, drinking, reciting poetry together and discussing his novel-in-progress.

"Yeah," said Butsy, "that's a way of looking at it!"

"Three cheers for Tod!" said Sophia, raising her voice and her glass.

And they all joined in, "Hip, hip, hurray! Hip, hip, hurray! Hip, hip, hurray!"

Sophia wasn't satisfied. "And three more for Grace, his amazing wife!"

II.

The long day's light had drained away. Now the apartment was illuminated by lamps and Christmas lights, which reflected on the brightly-colored ornaments and baubles that hung alongside chains of popcorn and glittering tinsel. The decorations lent the room a harsh, garish appearance, or so it seemed to Tod, but maybe it was just because his unexpected happy excitement had drained away like the day and his submerged but growing worry about Gracie's absence played at odds on his nerves. They had been drinking and talking for long hours. Music from the Big Band era filled the room. Jean and Butsy were dancing. Spring and Tod moved around them, struggling a little, trying to feel who would lead. Sophia looked on and tapped the floor with her cane.

Spring stopped suddenly and said, "Enough!" She turned away from Tod and sat back down at the table with Sophia.

Tod followed her. "Too much," he said.

Spring looked at the other couple and said, to Jean, "Isn't Butsy a wonderful dancer!"

"He certainly is," said Jean, "he's a dream!"

"I wonder where Grace is," Sophia said. "It's getting dark outside."

"Yes," said Jean, "and we've been at it for hours. Isn't anybody getting hungry?"

“Let’s bring out the food,” said Spring. “Gracie can eat when she gets here. She won’t mind if we don’t wait for her.”

Tod said, “I’d like to wait for her. She can’t be much longer.”

“Oh, she won’t mind, Tod. Help me, Jean. We’ll make a nice crabmeat salad.” Spring and Jean got up, went to the kitchenette and began putting together the cold cuts and salad spread.

“Your Mom just can’t wait for anybody, Tod. I’m always running after her. When I say, ‘Why can’t you wait for me?’—you know what she says? ‘I’m an individual.’ I don’t even know what she means. She’s really something! Ain’t she something, Tod.”

Sophia looked at Butsy and said, “Why?”

“Why what? Butsy asked.

“Why do you run after her?”

“Because I’m crazy about her. What do you think? She’s a free spirit. Don’t like to be pinned down.”

“That’s a bit irresponsible, isn’t it?” Sophia said.

“Hey, wait a minute,” said Butsy. “She don’t have to answer to nobody.”

“She doesn’t *have* to, but shouldn’t she? I know of several times when Tod has stopped working because he expected a visit from his mother and then she didn’t show up.” Sophia hit a sore spot. And she knew Tod well enough to know that it was true.

“That’s her business, ain’t it?”

“No. If you make an appointment and someone stops what he’s doing because of it and then you don’t meet him or call him up and explain, I’d say it had become his business. Tod is a writer. His work requires concentration and good work habits. It requires self-discipline, and that sort of thing is very distracting and weakening. Too much interruption can damage a work, or even damage the writer. I know. I write myself. And I wouldn't allow anyone to do that to me. Tod's patience amazes me."

Butsy looked over at Tod and said, "Is this old dame a good friend of yours?"

Spring had heard this little exchange and came back to the table and said to Sophia, "If I ever do that, it's between my son and me, and I'll thank you to mind your own business."

"Huh-oh," Tod said.

Sophia was undaunted. "Tod," she went on, "is a good son. I know how unhappy you sometimes make him, Spring. I've seen him put his very important work aside and sit in expectation of one of your visits, then you not show up. You don't seem to understand what it does to him."

By now all the drinks Spring had polished off during the afternoon were rising and carrying her to greater heights of . . . who knew? "Who are you?" Spring went on. "You have no business here anyway, you old drunkard."

Even Butsy seemed to think some cheer should be restored. "Don't get sore at the old douche-bag, Spring. What a temper! Ain't she something?"

"No! She can't talk to me like that in my son's house."

"Nevertheless, Mom, she's telling the truth. Suppose I had been working today. You had no way of knowing I wasn't, but you barge in anyhow, without any warning, and even bring company. I waited for you all day yesterday. And nobody showed up or even called. This has happened a thousand times."

"I've explained that."

"Your Mom explained that," said Butsy. "Remember, your mother is the best friend you'll ever have. I know my mother is."

"I don't know about your mother, Butsy, but mine has been driving me crazy ever since I can remember. That's what my novel is about—my playboy father and my merry widow mother. They were both so damned gay! Except when my father was staggering around for weeks on end in his shitty undershorts and my mother was screaming at him until I thought my eardrums would break. They were irresponsible, that's what they were! Selfish and irresponsible!"

Jean was listening and suddenly said, "I'm not so sure you have any right to talk about anybody being irresponsible, Tod. If you had been more responsible, maybe Billy would still be here." Then she was quiet and began to cry. Sophia and Spring gathered around her and tried to comfort.

Sophia said, "She's just had a little too much to drink, I think."

"Naw," Butsy said. "She *needs* a drink."

"Mister Butsy," Sophia said, "I wonder if you would be so kind as to go to the liquor store for me. If you would get me a pint of whiskey—I'd like to go to my own apartment." She waved out a bill from her dress pocket.

"Do it, Butsy. Get it for her," Spring said.

Suddenly, Jean stood up from the table, still crying. She pointed a finger at Tod and cried, "He killed my husband! He took him out and killed him!"

"You know damn well that isn't true, Jean!" Tod was hurt by the accusation, even though he knew she knew it wasn't true and it was just the booze.

"It is true! Billy had a wonderful career ahead of him, and now he's dead!"

"You know as well as I do that Billy was an alcoholic. He was reckless. He was picked up by the police where he had fallen many a time. He was always bruised and banged up from falling down somewhere."

"But you had him stay with you and drink that day and then you let him get away and die—"

"I was too drunk—"

"Well, isn't that irresponsible?"

"Well, aren't you drunk now? Didn't you ever drink with him? It just *happened* to happen when he was with me."

"Is that how you explain it to yourself?" She was calming down a bit now.

Tod hesitated and said, "No." No, he thought, he could never explain it to himself.

"She's just upset, Tod," Spring said. "She doesn't mean what she's saying."

"To hear you," Sophia said, "nobody means what he or she is saying. I can assure you that *I* generally do. But Jean doesn't *know* what she's saying."

Tod put his arm around Jean, and tried to make her look at him. "You know Billy's death wasn't any more my fault because he had gone out with me than it would have been your fault if he had gone out with you. You know that, Jean."

"He never died with me," she said quietly. "Somebody's got to be responsible for something!"

"Here, have another drink," said Spring. "Now drink it slowly."

"She should have some coffee," said Sophia. "Tod, why don't you recite a poem? It'll get her mind off it. Tod's a wonderful reader."

"Oh, I don't want to hear any of that," said Spring. "This is supposed to be a party."

Jean looked at the others and tried to dry her eyes with her sleeve, "No, let him," she said. "I like to listen to him recite. Billy always said Tod was a wonderful reader of poetry."

"I don't feel like it," Tod said.

"Please, Tod. I'm sorry for what I said. I don't know what comes over me. Billy loved to hear you read."

"It's boring," Spring sighed. "It's very boring when you are trying to have fun."

"Well," Sophia said, "it *is* his party. Recite something for us, Tod."

"Yeah—O.K. I've got just the number for this occasion." He went to the bookcase and pulled out a volume. He thumbed through it it and began:

"This is by Poe. It's called 'To My Mother—'"

"Is this going to be insulting?" Spring said. "Because if it is—"

"I don't see how anybody can be insulted by this. Why be defensive? Do you feel guilty?" He began to read:

"Because I feel that, in the heavens above,
The angels, whispering to one another,
Can find, among their burning terms of love,
None so devotional as that of 'Mother,'
Therefore by that dear name I long have called you—
You who are more than mother unto me,
And fill my heart of hearts, where Death installed you,
In setting my Virginia's spirit free.
My mother—my own mother, who died early,
Was but the mother of myself; but you
Are mother to the one I loved so dearly,
And thus are dearer than the mother I knew
By that affinity with which my wife
Was dearer to my soul than its soul life."

While Tod was reading, Butsy quietly opened the door and entered the room. He waited there, bottle in bag in hand, listening, and puffing on his cigar.

"Now that's the right way to talk to your mother," he said.

Sophia got up and went to meet Butsy, saying to Tod, "Thank you for that good reading, Tod. It was lovely!" She took the bag from Butsy and turned toward the door, tapping her cane.

"Your change," Butsy said, and handed it to Sophia.

"Please keep it for your trouble. Good evening. And congratulations again, Tod! I knew that wonderful novel would be snatched up by somebody." The door closed behind her.

"Keep it for my trouble!" said Butsy. "She gave me a tip, like I was an errand boy! The nerve of the old douche-bag!"

"Sit down, Butsy!" Spring said. "That poem was beautiful, Tod. Thank you."

"What for? I don't think you understood it, did you?"

"Now don't start on me again, just when I thought you'd stopped."

"You know," Butsy said, "that poem makes me think of how I haven't called my Mom in a long time. I think it's been a year. She's nearly ninety. She won't be around much longer."

"Now don't go getting sentimental. Let's have some fun, for God's sake! Put the dance music back on, Tod! I just love to dance, don't you, Jean?"

"I loved to dance with Billy. He was a wonderful dancer."

"How 'bout me?" Butsy said, looking at Jean.

"Butsy is a wonderful dancer," said Spring

"And red-headed, like Billy."

"Hey, Spring, is she flirting with me? Are you flirting with me, girly?"

"The vanity of men! You old fool, she's young enough to be your granddaughter!"

"My daughter, maybe. Don't forget, I'm a lot younger than you are."

"Oh, thanks a lot. But you aren't *that* much younger."

Butsy sat down at the table and said, "I can't stop thinking about my mother. It comes to me sometimes that maybe she's dead already, and I don't know it."

"Doesn't your brother live with her?" Spring said. "He'd tell you if anything had happened to her."

"Maybe not. I'm the bum in the family. They don't care what I know. The last time I saw my brother, I tried to put the touch on him for a few hundred—he's a contractor and he's got the money—and he wouldn't give me a dime. He tried to throw me out, but I bopped him one on the nose. I broke his beak for him, that's what I did. No; maybe he wouldn't tell me."

"I thought you were a jockey, not a boxer," said Jean.

"I fought feather weight in the Golden Gloves before I was a jockey."

"Was that before you were a stuntman?" she said.

"Yeah. But suppose Mamma's dead?"

"If you want to, you can call her up from here, Butsy. The phone's over there."

"Gee—thanks, Tod—but no. I'm afraid she might be dead. I don't want to know."

"That's just the way I felt when Billy was missing," Jean said.

"I was home, drunk, asleep," Tod said, thinking of Billy. "I didn't know until the next day. He was still alive, in intensive care, when I went to see him. Unconscious. He died a few hours later. I didn't want to know, either, when he died."

Spring said, "When my husband was missing—in the fire—I was glad when he wasn't immediately identified. There was a chance, then. But I knew he was dead. Tod finally identified him at the morgue."

"He was living in an old fire trap rooming house in Newark," Tod told Butsy and Jean. "It was filled with derelicts and drunks like himself. Six of them died."

"We had had an argument," Spring said, "and he had moved down there—but he would have come back as soon as he sobered up."

"He told me that he was never going back to you. He said he wanted some peace." Tod went on, speaking to Butsy, "He was an old man, much older than Mom is now, and that was five years ago. I was a late child. He had had another son, by a former marriage, and I don't think he ever really wanted me, though he loved me well enough in his way, I guess. I don't think he wanted to have any children by Mom. I was an accident."

"You were not!" Spring blurted. "He let me have you because I wanted you. He had had me aborted twice before."

"Jesus, Mary and Joseph, don't say it!" cried Butsy.

"He didn't mean it about not coming back," Spring said.

"He said you drove him crazy," Tod said.

"Well, he drove *me* crazy," said Spring.

"But he was drunk, Mom. You were sober by then. If you had only let him be, he wouldn't have gone to that firetrap to find some peace."

Butsy was lost in his own thoughts. "What if she's dead?" he said to no one. He began to cry. Jean had been sitting quietly and couldn't take all this revelatory madness. She got up and ran from the apartment. Tod started to go after her, but Spring said, "Let her go. She'll feel better if she gets it out of her system."

Butsy looked at Spring and said, "But what if my Mamma is dead?"

"She isn't dead!" Spring said.

"Call her up, Butsy," said Tod.

"It's long distance—California. But I'll pay for the call, Tod. Could I?"

"Sure. Go ahead."

Butsy sat down on the couch next to a small telephone table and took out his address book. He found the number and started to put the call through.

"Your father would have come back to me, and it was cruel of you to say that he wouldn't," Spring said to Tod.

"Cruel! Don't you think the things you do—and always have done—are cruel? All you ever say is how I took thirty-eight hours to be born, and how agonizing it was for you. You could start right there."

"Well, that's the truth!" Spring said.

"But do you still have to tell me it every time we have a drink together?"

"Well, what's it got to do with you? I was the one who was in pain."

"Because I didn't want to come out and meet you!"

"That's a rotten thing to say to your mother!"

Butsy got his line and asked into the phone, "Mamma? Mamma?"

Tod and Spring were oblivious to Butsy and his call. "You're just drunk!" Spring said. "You've turned out to be a drunk like your father."

"How else could I turn out? It's all I've ever known."

Butsy jerked around on the couch and faced Spring and Tod. "She's dead! She's dead, Spring! What?" He listened again to the phone.

"You should respect your mother!" Spring shouted at Tod.

"There's nothing to respect!" he shouted back at her.

"Please, somebody—my Mamma's dead! What? What?" Butsy strained to hear someone at the end of the line.

"Oh, for God's sake! Help him, Tod. Stop *crying* Butsy! Tod, take that phone away from him!"

Tod took the phone from Butsy and said into it, "I'm a friend of—what? Oh, I see. Yes. Yes, he's had a few." Tod put his hand over the mouthpiece and said, "Butsy, your mom is in bed. She's fine. She's taking a nap. Here—" Then he handed the phone back to Butsy.

"Hello?" Butsy said, speaking again into the phone.

Spring sat down at the table and said to Tod, "I don't know why you hate me so much. I've always been a good mother."

Tod could not believe what he heard. He said, "Which is why I was dragged all over the country and never got any schooling. You should have seen to it that I was taken care of. It was your responsibility. People have no right to have a kid and then to just pretend he isn't there."

"That was your father's fault. I had to go where he went. I didn't have any money. Other women have had it easier."

“Other women have worked and worked like dogs. You could have worked. You could have made a real home for us, even if it was just a little apartment.

Spring said, wearily, “What’s the use of re-hashing all this now? That’s all in the past.”

“No, it isn’t. It’s in the present. I’m still paying for it.”

“Have you forgotten what this party is about? Your novel is going to be published. You’re successful, so what difference does it make or not make what I did or didn’t do?”

“It makes a difference that I’ve been a nervous wreck all my life. That I haven’t been suited for a normal life. That I’m an alcoholic. That I’ve never been able to get a decent job. That, if this novel hadn’t been accepted, eventually I would have . . . killed myself.”

“Don’t say that! You’re just being dramatic!”

“You damned old selfish insensitive bitch! All you’ve ever cared about was some paltry comfort and a good time to break the monotony!”

Butsy finished his phone call and was apparently relieved. “Mamma’s alive! I talked to her!” he said.

At that moment, the apartment door swung open and Grace came in, carrying bundles. She was shocked, seeing the Christmas decorations and dim lights. “Well, what’s happening here?” she said. “What is this, a party?” Then, seeing Spring, “Hello, Mom!” She saw Butsy and said, smiling, “Hello, there.”

“Gracie, this is my friend, Fred Suddeth. Fred, my daughter-in-law, Gracie.”

“Call me Butsy.” He held out his cigar and pointed to it.

"Hello, Butsy!" she said, still wondering what was going on.

"Gracie, sit down! I've got great news!" said Tod. "The greatest!"

Spring broke in—"Tod's novel has been accepted. Isn't it wonderful?"

Grace sat down and tried to take in the news. She was flustered and it dissolved into sheer joy. "Oh, Tod, it's true, isn't it? Honey, we did it! I can't believe it! Tell me all about it! What's happened?"

"Jerry called him this morning," Spring said. "He's got Tod a five thousand dollar advance."

"Money! We've even got money! Oh, Tod, I'm so proud of you!" Grace put her arms around Tod and kissed him.

"Would you like a drink, Gracie?" Spring offered.

"Wow! You know, Mom, I think I will have one for once—to celebrate. Tod's always complaining that I don't drink with him. Well, this is an occasion! Did you tell Sophia and Jean?" Then she said to Butsy, "They're our neighbors. And our best friends."

"They were here. Jean did the decorating," Tod said. "Like it?"

Grace looked around the room and said, "She must have had one too many."

"And I did the cleaning," Spring said.

"Oh, thanks so much, Mom. The place really does look festive. Well, cheers!"

"Cheers!" Spring and Butsy echoed.

"To you, honey!" Tod said, "for believing in me like nobody else ever has!"

"Oh, that's meant for me," said Spring.

"You shouldn't be mean to your Mom, Tod. Look how good I feel because my mother is alive. She's nearly ninety!"

"She was probably a good mother," said Tod.

They all sat down at the table and Butsy said, "She done her best. My old man was a beast. He threw me out when I was fourteen."

"I thought it was your brother."

"That was later. I already had practice by that time. That's what I said to my brother before I broke his beak; I said I should be doin' this to the old man." Butsy laughed, and went on, "I just now asked my brother on the phone how his nose feels, does it still hurt—I hope. But what could my mother do?"

"Well, she could have stopped him from throwing you out at fourteen," said Tod.

"Naw, them were different times."

"All times should be the same when it comes to that," Tod said.

"What's this all about?" Grace said. "Have I missed something?"

"He's picking on me again," said Spring.

"You shouldn't pick on Spring, Tod," said Butsy. "Just look at her! Ain't she cute? Ain't she something? I love that woman! She's a real individual! I love your mother, Tod. I don't think you should pick on her."

"It's between us."

"No, it isn't. Not when I'm here."

Grace stood up. "Now wait, both of you!" she said.

"Why don't you both just get out!" Tod shouted.

"All right," Spring said, "I'll be glad to go."

"You aren't even supposed to be here, you know. You were supposed to be here yesterday!"

"I can't let you act like this, Tod. I want you to apologize to Spring," said Butsy.

"Go to hell!"

Before anyone could stop them the two men were in a drunken shoving match. Tod lost his balance and fell to the floor. His head struck with a loud crack. Grace dropped to her knees beside him and lifted his bleeding head to her lap.

"Tod! Tod! Wake up!"

"Your dress is all blood! He's bleeding!" cried Spring.

"Christ, I'm sorry! Heads bleed something awful. But he's O.K."

` "It's his ears," Grace cried. "There's blood coming out of his ears! Oh, God! Tod? Tod? Wake up, honey!"

"Lemme see." Butsy squatted down and put his hand over Tod's heart. He looked up at the women. "I don't feel it. Christ, he's dead, I think! Christ, Spring, I didn't do nothing but push him. I didn't mean it. You know I didn't mean it. Jesus, Mary and Joseph! Oh, Christ!" Butsy jumped up and ran from the apartment.

"Call the hospital!" Spring cried out hysterically. "Do something! Somebody, do something!"

Grace sat on the floor rocking Tod's dead head in her lap.

PART IV.

WINNERS

Skulls seem to take pride in their bald hollowness, like grinning Halloween pumpkins. Have you ever seen one roll down from the top of a pile, like those piles that Pol Pot used to stack? Vanity-free, it is no less content at the bottom than it was at the top. It may rest there, upside down, and frown; but, right side up, it would still be wearing the same silly smile: all that is needed for you to see that smile is for you to stand on your head, or, to set it upright. And all skulls look pretty much alike. Some are a little elongated, some are flat on top, or bullet-shaped, but they are all pretty much the same, when unsupported by spines, and fallen to the lowest point of gravity's pull. Always they smile inanely, like poor country folk who have won the lottery. "Cheer up," they seem to say, "the best is yet to come."

HAYDN'S HEAD: A PASTICHE

for Jack O'Brian, columnist, New York Journal-American, who tipped me off

We are aboard the Orange Blossom Special, returning to New York from Florida, and I am hopeful that Tweedledum and Tweedledee, as Johnny calls them, a couple of bad eggs in plaid suits, are not.

"Odds are we've left them shaking their fists on the station platform, Pug," Johnny says, mopping his brown brow with a white silk handkerchief. He gears his seat back, loosens his tie, tips his Panama over his eyes, and acts like he hasn't got a worry in the world. I act like I am watching the midnight Miami lights recede, but what I am really doing is watching the window for reflections. I expect to see Sam the Elephant's bonebreakers appear at any second.

Most gamblers have a specialty—cards, craps, horses—but Johnny Belmont will bet on anything. I have first heard of him a year ago, when he places a spectacular bet on the presidential election and loses to all concerned. He is in deep trouble until his rich family steps in. But they are very much put out, because he has bet on Stevenson and they are an Eisenhower family. So they warn Johnny that they will not rescue him again. At least this is the version I have heard outside of Lindy's restaurant, in that vague area of the environment around Broadway and Fiftieth Street which Damon Runyon has dubbed Jacobs' Beach in honor of his ticket speculating pal, Mike Jacobs. On Jacobs' Beach you meet the sporting crowd—scalpers, bookies, touts, mobsters, and journalists such as Walter Winchell and, until he passes on in '46, Runyon himself.

But it is at Hialeah that Johnny and I have become pals. The Florida sharks do not know that Johnny is a black sheep without a red cent; so, with his good looks, his classy manners, and his family name, he has been able to borrow large amounts of hay from Sam the Elephant, who is called such because he does not forget so easy. But Johnny has been having the world's worst losing streak, and has tried to get on the good side of Lady Luck by placing some bets for me. Unfortunately, Sam the Elephant has heard of said bets; and, because he does not care from which individual he collects, has decided to hold me partners with Johnny when he calls in the bets.

We are tap city when we step off the Special at Penn Station—unless you count Johnny's lucky two-bit piece, which he never spends. But Johnny thinks we can get a stake at the Hotel Bon Chance, a gamblers' haven in the West Forties. I figure he means to check us in and flip his quarter into wealth. But I am worried that some of Sam the Elephant's boys might be keeping their eyes out for us there. Johnny laughs kind of grimly and says that we will have to gamble on that because the Bon Chance is the only place he can think of where he can raise a stake.

It looks like we are going to have to hoof it through a cold November rain, which is pouring out of buckets. It does not matter much to me, because I am not a dude, but it matters to Johnny, who is a clotheshorse. We have had to leave all our clothes in Florida, and he only has this one tropical suit left, which is on his back. So he shakes his head, and says: "Pug, I'm not going to let this suit get soaked."

I follow him through the crowd and up to the Lost and Found, which is open all night in those days, and it is now about midnight, as our trip takes us about twenty-four hours, and he tells the busy clerk behind the counter that he has lost his black umbrella. The clerk hustles off and is back in no time with three such. "That's it," cries Johnny, and takes the one that happens to be the best of the lot.

As we are walking away, Johnny says, "You know, Pug, one could get anything that way." He stops and looks at me with his green eyes bright like two Go signs. "Think of something, I'll bet you a belated C-note that they have it—that the clerk will hand it across to you."

There is nothing like a wager to cheer me up, and I need cheering. "You're on," I say. "We'll make it for the first C-note one of us gets."

"O.K.," says Johnny. "But I choose the item. It can't be anything with an I.D., and it can't be anything too unusual—like a zither. Fair enough?"

"Fair enough," I say, wondering what a zither is.

"Say a plain square box—a cardboard carton or package wrapped in plain brown paper and tied with twine—O.K.?"

"You're on."

"You ask for it. I got the umbrella. The clerk might remember me." On the 5-yard line from the Lost and Found desk, Johnny says: "I'll wait here." In two minutes I am back, carton in hand.

"I owe you a C-note," I say, dangling the package from a finger by the twine. "The bet's good," I add, and say that I will now return the package.

"Wait a minute, Pug," says Johnny. "How about another C-note on what's in it? Let's say on whether it's animal, vegetable, or mineral."

I say, "It's bigger than a breadbox, that's for sure."

"Takers?" says Johnny.

I shrug. "Takers," I say. "So where do we open it?"

"Not here," says Johnny. "I'll tell you what, Pug. We'll take it with us to the Bon Chance, and open it there. Then I'll have a boy re-wrap it and bring it back here to the Lost and Found. What do you say?"

"I suppose you want I should carry it?"

"And I'll keep us dry with the umbrella. Come on."

The Bon Chance is a few blocks uptown from Penn Station. Cats and Dogs of rain are bouncing knee-high as we turn off the avenue. On the next corner is a Yellow Cab stand, or used to be in those days. I duck to look into the first cab in the line and there as usual is Sleeping Bill, who could make a claim to being the worst hack in New York, as he never takes a fare. Actually, it is his own car, done up to look like a Yellow Cab, and he is no hack at all, but a bookie. I tap his windshield but he is asleep at the wheel. I think he has been so since I left for Florida. Anyway, he's in the same position he was in when I left.

In a block or two on this numbered cross-street the pedestrian traffic has thinned down to Johnny and me. Ahead, through the watery dark I see *BON CHANCE* come and go in nervous green neon winks. I am looking at this sign, and thinking about a hot bath, when a dark, shiny limo sprays up beside us. The back window on our side is rolled down and there is the head of a white-faced, dark-hatted woman in it. She has thin red lips and big white teeth through which she hisses something at us, which I cannot make out due to the fact that the rain is doing drum rolls. A big boy in a chauffeur's uniform comes around from the other side. He is waving a revolver which has a silencer on it like a rolled-up racing form. He believes that action speaks louder than words, because instead of explaining himself he hooks a couple of thick fingers into the twine on the box I am conveying and tugs. I tug back. He then swings at me and misses, but corrects himself by bashing the big silencer down on my knuckles. Only now does he decide to make himself clear.

"Let go, you fat swine!" he cries, adding insult to injury. But before I can be offended, Johnny has collapsed the umbrella and batted it down on the pistol, which splashes into a jumping lake at the rear end of the limo.

"En garde!" cries Johnny, stabbing the guy several short ones. The big guy lets go of the twine, and slips in the rain just as I step in with a right cross. He falls against the limo and keeps on going down toward where the pistol has submerged, slapping at street water, grabs up the pistol, aims, and pulls the trigger.

Because of the silencer and the noise of the rain, I don't know if I have been shot or not, but then I realize by the look on the big guy's face that the pistola is water-logged.

Johnny and I have jumped away when he has had the pistola pointed at us, so he has a head start when he ducks around the limo. The door slams and the limo speeds off, making a wake like the Titanic.

"What the hell . . ." says Johnny, looking after the limo.

"It is this dumb package," I say.

"Did you see the plates?" says Johnny. "They were diplomatic. Let's get to a room and see what we've got here."

There is a new night clerk at the Bon Chance, a straw-haired, freckled kid with a Southern accent. This is a break, as the old clerk would have sold out his mother to Sam the Elephant or any other shark for the price of a warm beer. It won't help much if Sam the Elephant's boys are looking hard for us, but it is anyway worth the ink to register under a couple of phony names, so we do. A kid who looks like the younger brother of the yokel behind the desk shows us up, carrying the package by the twine, like a suitcase.

In our room, Johnny offers to flip the kid double or nothing for the tip, neglecting to state the amount involved, and the kid eagerly takes the bet. Johnny then offers to let the kid owe him "the ten spot." But before the kid has about-faced, Johnny has flipped him into serious debt, which he immediately cancels, on the condition that we get top service, to which the kid gratefully agrees.

Johnny orders sandwiches, coffee, cigarettes, cigars, razors, etc. He also needs a bottle of good Scotch.

He sends the kid away with our wet clothes. In those days, you can get a good steam press all night, even in a cheap hotel.

"Well, now, Pug," says Johnny, ripping open the package, "let's have a look at this."

I go over to the table on which the kid has placed the box and look into it. Johnny is pulling out a lot of excelsior. There is something round and gray down in the middle of the box. Johnny pulls more excelsior out, reaches in, and jerks back like he's been stung. I see it now and let out a whistle. It is a human skull.

As soon as it sinks in what we have here, we do a thorough search of the box for identification of some kind—"Provenance," Johnny calls it—even checking inside the skull, but discover zero. We pack the bony head away; and then, while we bathe and shave, we discuss the nature of things as they stand.

We ask ourselves: Who are the foreign couple in the limo? Why do they want this old skull? Should we call the police?

Johnny says, combing his dark hair down over his forehead and cutting a part in it, "Do the chauffeur and his lady know that the package contains a skull, rather than something else more valuable? Surely an ordinary human skull can't be worth much. Surely not enough to induce armed robbery."

Comes a rapping at our chamber door.

"Who is it?" Johnny calls.

"Bellboy. I got your clothes and a wagon full of food and drinks."

When the bellboy goes, Johnny says, "Get dressed, Pug," and pulls on his pants.

I am tying my tie in the cloudy mirror over the dresser when there is a second knock at the door.

"What now?" Johnny calls over the transom. He thinks it is the bellboy again.

"Please," comes a reply. "I am Professor-Doctor Albrecht Schmitt with my daughter, Agnes. We have rooms down the hall. I must speak with you."

"It don't sound like anybody Sam the Elephant would know," I say.

"Nor like the chauffeur from the limo," says Johnny. He opens the door a crack and peers out. Then he steps back and opens it wide.

This gent has a couple of inches on me and I have a couple of pounds on him, making us two barrels, but his weight is then as old as mine is now, and he has never been a lightweight boxer as I have before I lose my last match in the late 40's and begin consoling myself with pumpkin pies.

He has a gray, yellow-streaked walrus mustache, and thick, silver-rimmed specs. His daughter is taller and a hundred pounds lighter, a honey-blonde in powder blue who looks like a wicked witch has chased her out of a fairy tale. She eyes Johnny like he is Prince Charming.

The gent extends a thin manicured hand. "I'm Professor-Doctor Schmitt," he repeats. Gray moths flutter behind his specs. "I see you have opened our package. We were on our way up from Washington with that skull when we suspected we were being followed. You see, it is a valuable specimen, and there are those who would stop at nothing to possess it. Research is highly competitive. You Americans have a phrase—*it's a jungle*." He gives out with a nervous cackle.

Johnny lights a Fatima. He says, "It hasn't got a name or a number on it. How do we know it's yours?"

The Doc looks stumped. The gray moths look like they are trying to break out from behind their glass cages.

Johnny purses his lips, lifting his little black mustache, and blows out some Turkish smoke, giving Agnes the once-over twice. She looks at him with big sad blue eyes. He cracks a smile. "Maybe you can tell me how you lost it—?"

"Oh, no," the Doc almost stutters, "it wasn't lost. Just as we were leaving the train, we became *certain* that we were being followed. But we hoped we had lost our pursuers in the crowd when we came upon a row of lockers. Unfortunately, neither of us had an appropriate coin—"

"We had to work fast," Agnes breaks in. "In a moment's inspiration, my father saw the Lost and Found, and we deposited it there."

"Then," the Doc picks up, "we waited nearby to make certain that our pursuers had not seen us turn in the package."

"You can imagine," says Agnes, "our surprise when we saw—you, Mr.—"

"Morris," I say. "Pug Morris."

"—Mr. Morris, pick up the package."

"You were not at all what we were looking for in our pursuers," says the Doc.

"Sorry," I say, as I am pulling the ring from a Prince Albert.

"No, no," says the Doc, kind of flustered. "I did not mean—"

"Frankly," pipes Agnes, "we thought you might be some sort of confidence tricksters who preyed on Lost and Found patrons."

"If that should prove to be the case," says the Doc, kind of shrugging, "I'm certain that we can come to terms—"

This time I break in. "We picked up the package on a lark," I say, around my stogie, which I am busy lighting.

"We're gamblers," Johnny says. He explains the bet.

"I see," says the Doc, when Johnny has finished. "We followed when you left the station, and saw the assault on you. We should certainly have helped, for those who attempted to steal the package from you were assuredly those who pursued us from Washington, but I'm getting old, and the rain was beating down, and we had fallen too far behind to be of any assistance."

"They must have found us," says Agnes, "and then seen you ahead of us with the package, passed us by, and attacked—"

"We saw you turn in here," says the Doc.

"We told the clerk we were friends of yours and wanted rooms on your floor," says Agnes. "We've been drying off and making ourselves presentable."

"Now," says the Doc, "if you'd please be so kind as to give us our package . . ."

Johnny grins, and says: "We still don't know that the package is yours. Maybe it belongs to the pair who jumped us."

"Yeah," I say, "and maybe everything you've told us is a load of—"

"Pug!" says Johnny.

"—baloney," I say.

Schmitt's face falls. He thinks for a moment, and says, in a much more businesslike manner, "We haven't much time, gentlemen," reaches into a breast pocket, pulls out a fat wallet, and takes a couple of bills from it. "Will a hundred—er, two hundred—one each—be satisfactory?"

"Mister," I say, "we lose more than that before breakfast."

But Johnny takes the two bills, stuffs one in his pocket, and, handing me the other, says, "Here, Pug, cash this and call the cops."

I start for the phone, but the Doc cries, "Stop!" When I turn back, he is holding a .30 Mauser, with its little black eye looking right at me. "Put your hands up and hand me that box," he orders.

"Which is it, Professor?" says Johnny in his usual cheerful way, his hands half up, talking through the smoke from his dangling Fatima.

"Agnes," says Schmitt, "get the head."

Now we are all startled. Someone is at our door again.

"We are very popular tonight, Johnny," I say.

"Infamously, Pug," says Johnny.

Neck on neck, Johnny knocks the Mauser to the floor and I catch the Doc on the chin with a light fast uppercut.

Schmitt has gone down across the coffee wagon, taking a few items with him. In short, he has made a good deal of noise. Plus which, Agnes has screamed.

"It could be the Elephant's boys," I say.

Johnny grabs up the Doc's Mauser, looks sharp at Agnes, finger to lips, and steps to the wall by the door so he will be behind it when it opens. He nods at me.

I stay put and call, "Come in!"

It is the chauffeur and the pale-faced lady from the limo. The chauffeur is holding the revolver with the big silencer on it. The gat looks dry and newly oiled.

I back up some toward the table with the package on it, drawing them in. They bite, and step in, eyeing Agnes and the Doc's unconscious bulk.

"Where's the other—?"

But the chauffeur has got curious too late. Johnny jams the Doc's Mauser into his back.

"Well," says Johnny, "if it isn't my fencing partner! Drop it."

The chauffeur drops the big revolver with a thud. Johnny kicks the door shut behind him, steps around in front, and kicks the gat to the side.

"Who are you two?" he asks, pleasantly.

The chauffeur clicks his heels. "Colonel Ivan Lensky," he says, "Soviet State Security. This is my associate, Frau Yeva Von Heller of Austria."

"KGB," says Johnny. "How interesting. My uncle is Wild Bill Belmont."

"OSS," says Lensky. "I have met him. A double-dyed conservative McCarthyite reactionary."

"That's Uncle Bill," says Johnny, smiling.

"Who are you talking about?" I say.

"Spies!" says Johnny.

"We already know Doctor Schmitt and his daughter," says Lensky. "Who are you?"

"Not-so-innocent bystanders," says Johnny. "Gamblers who made a bet on a live lark and wound up with a dead head."

"That head is important to Frau Von Heller and myself—to the governments we represent. We are prepared to offer you two thousand dollars. I have on my person an instrument for that amount. Payment cannot be stopped."

"Two *grand*," I say. "That might keep the Elephant from our door, Johnny."

"Elephant?" The Colonel looks intrigued.

"An Americanism," says Johnny. He looks at Agnes, who frowns, and at the Doc, who groans, and at me, who shrugs. "Make it five thousand," he says.

"Ah," sighs Lensky. "It so happens—"

"That you have another instrument for five thousand," says Johnny.

Frau Von Heller says: "We represent the rightful owners."

The Colonel waves a hammy hand at Agnes and the Doc. "These two are frauds."

"No," cries the Doc, looking up from the floor, "don't give it to them! You would be betraying your country. It doesn't belong to them and you cannot put a money value on it. It's priceless!"

Now come more knocks. It is like a convention.

"House detective," comes a voice. "Open up!"

"No deal," says Johnny to Lensky and Von Heller, who have closed ranks. Lensky whispers something in Von Heller's ear.

"Shut up, you two," I say. "And behave."

"Open up!" says the dick outside the door.

“Get your father up,” Johnny says to Agnes.

A key is inserted in the lock.

“He’s got a key, Johnny,” I say. “It’s the house dick, all right.”

Johnny shoves the Mauser in his belt at the small of his back and drops his coat tail over it. He pulls open the door, a ring of keys jangling on the other side of the lock.

“What the hell—” says the house dick. He is long and thin in a worn blue suit and looks at us from a long thin yellow face, sour as kraut. “Why didn’t you open up?” he asks, scowling.

“There’s been an accident,” says Johnny. “We were busy.”

“What’s going on in here?” says the dick. “Folks down the hall say they heard noise and screaming. You realize it’s two in the morning?” He gives me a hard look. “Hey, wait a minute. Ain’t you Pug Morris?”

“You got me,” I say.

“You ain’t registered, Morris. Who’s he?” he asks, spotting the Doc.

“He’s my father,” says Agnes, rising from the floor where she’s been trying to get the Doc up. “He fainted and knocked over the tray and the lamp and I cried out. He’s been suffering this condition for some time, but I’m still terribly upset and was caught off guard when it happened. I’m sorry we disturbed the other patrons.”

I notice now that Frau Von Heller has her big black hat off. The house dick has stepped in close to get a good look at the Doc, and Von Heller and Lensky are edging toward the door.

"You're not leaving?" says Johnny, like a disappointed host.

"Duty calls," says Lensky. "I hope you and Mr. Morris will reconsider our offer."

"Ah!" cries Von Heller. She has dropped her hat. It is pretty obvious to everybody but the house dick, who has his back to her, that she has scooped up the big revolver with the hat.

"Keep your powder dry," I say.

She touches her pale cheek with a red nail, says, "Yes, it's still raining," turns on Lensky's arm, and the pair step out of the room; and, I hope, out of my life, but I doubt it.

"Everything here all right then?" asks the dick. "Want me to get a doctor for your father, miss?"

"No," says Agnes. "It isn't serious. And my father's a doctor."

Schmitt sits up and shakes his head. "I'm getting too old for this work," he says.

"I'd better help Father to his room," says Agnes.

"I'll help you with him," says Johnny.

"Wait a minute," says the dick. "Don't I know you, too? Ain't you Johnny Belmont?"

"Clarence Feathergale," says Johnny. "It's on the register."

"Feathergale! Well, Feathergale, *I'll* help the young lady and her father. The Bon Chance don't want no lawsuit on its hands."

"I'll be back when Father is comfortable," says Agnes, "to explain."

Johnny pushes the door after them, leaving it ajar.

"That dick has us pegged," I say. "He'll tip the Elephant's boys for sure."

"Maybe not," says Johnny. "Maybe he doesn't want any trouble here on his carpeted beat. In any case, we'll have to gamble that he doesn't. We can't walk out on a situation like this, Pug. That young lady needs help, and maybe our country needs help—and maybe there's enough money somewhere in this situation to pay off Sam the Elephant and to get us a new stake."

"So what makes an old skull so valuable?" I say.

Johnny snaps his fingers. "Pug," he says, "maybe it's not *what*, but *who*."

This gives us something to think about while we straighten up the room. We set the wagon up, put what is unbroken back on top, and I fix us a couple of drinks. I call down for the boy to clean up the mess on the rug and bring us some fresh sandwiches. When he has gone we finally put some food aboard. I am several meals behind.

As I'm swallowing the last corner of the last sandwich, Agnes taps and steps in.

"How's your father?" says Johnny.

"All right," she says. "He's resting. But he really shouldn't be doing this."

"Doing what, exactly?" says Johnny.

"This kind of work—for the government."

"It's on the level, then?" I say. "Listen, Miss Schmitt, I am really sorry that I have to deck him, see, but I want to make sure that he comes loose from that Mauser."

"He understands," she says. "He shouldn't have drawn the gun. It was an act of desperation. Oh, why on earth did you pick up that package! How did you *know* about it?"

"We didn't know," I say. "It was just a wild bet."

"Then, you really *are* gamblers?"

"You do not know the half of it, lady," I say. "We are even now being chased by loan sharks who will bite off our legs if we do not paddle."

"You're not criminals?"

"My name, Miss Schmitt," says Johnny, "is Belmont. I come from a long line of generals and statesmen. A good third of my family is in government—the other two-thirds are in money."

"Then you're patriots?"

"Black sheep, but true blue," says Johnny, with plenty of pride, "and with wounds to prove it."

"Johnny made a hero of himself fighting Hitler," I say. "That's how come he ain't in Korea. War wounds. And he has the medals to prove it."

"Well," says Agnes, impressed. "Perhaps you'll fix me a drink. I'm a little unsteady."

I fix the three of us some Scotch and soda and we settle down to hear what she has to say.

"Do you know anything about Austria?" she begins.

"Nope," I say.

Johnny just sips his Scotch.

"It's divided," she says, "Into American, British, French, and Russian zones. Vienna is in the Russian zone, but the Inner City is administered by each power in turn for a month, and patrolled day and night by groups of four soldiers drawn from the Four Powers."

"Sounds complicated," I say.

"It is," she says. "There are hopes for reunification, even plans ongoing. But things *can* go wrong."

"Well, what has this got to do with the head?" I say.

"My father and I are agents for the forces in and out of Austria who oppose Communism. That skull may become important—even more important—if reunification fails. You see, it is the skull of one of the greatest composers who ever lived—an Austrian named Franz Josef Haydn."

"What did I tell you, Pug," chirps Johnny, beaming. "It's *who*." He leaps up and digs the skull out, palms it, and says, like an actor: "Alas, poor Haydn! I love his music!"

He sits down with the skull in his lap.

"Then you may know," Agnes goes on, "that Haydn died in Eighteen-nine. Austria was at war with France then. A battle was advancing into Vienna. Haydn was buried in the middle of that battle. The local prison chief, a man named Peter, was an amateur phrenologist—"

"What is that?" I say.

"One who studies the conformation of the skull to divine mental faculties," says Johnny.

I guess he can see that I have missed him.

"They study the bumps on your head to see what you're like," he explains.

"They would think that I am pretty complicated," I say, "what with all my bumps."

"Extremely complicated," says Johnny.

"And so," Agnes picks up, "in the middle of all the confusion of the battle, the prison chief, Peter, had the body exhumed, and the head cut off. He stripped the head of all flesh, studied the skull, and finally pronounced that Haydn had the bumps of music fully developed."

"And what if he hadn't?" asks Johnny, smiling. "Would this Peter have cancelled his season ticket?"

"I don't know," says Agnes, laughing. "Anyway, he had planned to return the skull, but had taken too long in his study of it, and now felt that returning it was too dangerous. Instead, he had an ebony, glass-windowed box made, which he had decorated with a golden lyre. The skull was placed in this box, on a white silk cushion trimmed with black.

"But Peter lived in fear of being caught with it, and later passed it on to a man named Rosenbaum, who was secretary to Haydn's patron, Prince Esterhazy. Prince Esterhazy was, of course, unaware of all this, until he decided to give Haydn a more dignified burial than the one he had during the war; and, in course, had the coffin brought to him at Eisenstadt, the capital of Burgenland, in East Austria, where Haydn had lived under his patronage, and opened. The Prince was horrified to discover that there was only a wig where the head should have been. He investigated, and traced the decapitation to the prison chief, Peter. He was furious, and sent the police to Peter, who confessed his deed, and that Rosenbaum now had the skull. The Prince demanded that the head be returned. Rosenbaum returned a skull. The Prince had it examined and identified as the skull of a twenty year old man. Haydn died at Seventy-seven. Now the Prince had a search made of Rosenbaum's house, but it did not yield any result, as Rosenbaum's wife, the singer

Therese Gassmann, had hidden the skull in her straw mattress and lay on her bed during the search.

"It was Frau Rosenbaum who was behind Rosenbaum's refusal to return the skull. The glass and ebony display case containing that gruesome relic you're holding had become the highlight of her famous musical evenings.

"Then the Prince tried bribery. His emissaries promised Rosenbaum a huge sum if he would deliver the skull. Whereupon the besieged Rosenbaum bought the skull of an old man from a Vienna mortuary. This skull was much closer in phrenological detail to Haydn's, and was accepted as the original and interred with Haydn's body.

"On his deathbed, Rosenbaum bequeathed the real skull back to prison chief Peter, who in turn bequeathed it to the Society of Friends of Music in Vienna, who owned a great number of Haydn relics. But Peter's wife gave it to her doctor instead, who presented it to the Austrian Institute of Pathology and Anatomy in Eighteen Thirty-Two. They supposedly passed it on to the Society of Friends of Music, to whom it was originally willed by Peter.

"In Nineteen Thirty-Two, Prince Paul Esterhazy—direct descendant of Haydn's patron—promised to build a magnificent tomb for Haydn, if the head were restored to the body. But, while the authorities were still discussing the matter, the Second World War erupted. As a result of new political divisions after the war, Haydn's skeleton lay in the Soviet Zone while his skull rested in the International Zone. All of this is public knowledge; but of how the skull was stolen and taken to the Soviet

Zone, then retrieved by agents of the Western democracies, nothing has been made public. The world in general still believes the real skull to be in the possession of the Society of Friends of Music, in Vienna. Both the democracies and the forces of Communism would like to claim the genius for their own, but neither can, until skull and skeleton are reunited. No price can be put upon the propaganda value of such a coup."

"And this is the real head?" I say.

"Yes," says Agnes, "and the Communists know it. If they get it, they will have Haydn."

"How did it get to the States?" says Johnny.

"That remains a classified secret," says Agnes. "But it's my father's job to get it back to Vienna."

"Why didn't they send it on a battleship?" I say.

"Classified," says Agnes. "But let me say this much. It's not generally realized that the skull in Vienna is a fake, as I've said. So everything has to be done—unobtrusively." She studies us for a moment, then says: "The head is priceless because you can't put a price on propaganda value, but there *is* financial value attached to it. The authorities are offering twenty-five thousand dollars to anyone who is of assistance in recovering the head. So, if you'll help us, you wouldn't be doing it for nothing."

I look at Johnny. His green eyes are very bright.

"I can explain a little further," says Agnes. "There are two other skulls being pursued right now—bogus skulls—one in Europe and one in Asia. They are meant to confuse the Communists."

"Two phonies," I say, "and we have the real one. Just like three card monte, eh, Johnny?"

“What do you want us to do?” says Johnny.

“There’s a freighter leaving at four this morning from Pier Ten. We want to be on it and at sea before Von Heller and Lensky or anyone else knows. If you and Mr. Morris could get us safely to it . . .”

“Why not a plane?” I say.

“The Captain is our associate. The few other passengers will have been closely screened and will present us with no problems. It’s all been arranged, you see. We were supposed to go directly to the ship from Penn Station. Your intervention—”

“Threw your plans off,” says Johnny. “Of course we’ll help. Pug, would you wrap up Maestro Haydn’s head, please. Here, let’s have one more drink for the road, then we’ll go down the hall and collect your father and see how we can get safely to Pier Ten.”

In a few minutes we are standing in front of Doc Schmitt’s door. Agnes raps on it lightly, calling:

“Father! Father!”

When no answer comes, Agnes opens the door.

The Doc is stretched out on the carpet. He faces the ceiling, open-eyed.

Agnes runs over and shakes him. “Father! Father!” she cries. She looks back at Johnny, her face twisting with grief. Johnny goes to her, bends down, feels the Doc’s pulse, listens for his heart, but it’s all automatic, as the old man’s eyes keep staring up, like he’s looking through the ceiling at the stars. Johnny takes a shoulder and turns him over.

“He’s been stabbed,” he says.

“Not shot?” I say.

“There’s a slit in the back of his coat, not a hole.”

"Stabbed in the back," I say. "The dirty cowards."

"But why not shot?" says Johnny, like he's talking to himself.

"Noise," I say.

Johnny gives me an impatient look.

Agnes falls across the Doc's body in a dead faint. It must be delayed reaction. Johnny carries her to an easy chair, gets a damp towel from the bathroom, and pats her cheeks and forehead. Pretty soon she opens her eyes, which look bigger and bluer and sadder than ever. Johnny perches on the arm of her chair and puts an arm around her shoulders, which are shaking. She buries her face in his chest and in ten seconds his suit is wetter than it got in the rain. Finally she pulls back and says: "I shouldn't have left him alone . . ."

"Shouldn't we call the cops?" I say.

"No," says Johnny. "They'll tie us up and we've got to make that ship." He thinks for a minute, then says: "We've got to leave things as they are—for the time being. It's what your father would have wanted, Agnes."

"Yes," says Agnes, wiping her eyes. "He would want me to carry on with the mission. I must pull myself together—for him. What time is it?"

"Nearly three," I tell her.

She says: "And the ship weighs anchor at four o'clock this morning."

"Won't it wait for you?" I say.

"No," she says, shaking her head. "It's to leave without us. The Captain is to assume that we've failed."

"And if you fail," I say, "it will be our fault. Maybe this will cure you of making these wild bets,

Johnny," I add, feeling pretty bad about the whole thing. "Now maybe we have even hurt Uncle Sam."

Johnny says: "This must have happened a few minutes ago, when Agnes was in our room. That means that Lensky and Von Heller aren't very far away. Pug," he says, "take Agnes back to our room. Give her a drink. I'll be right along."

"What are you going to do?" I say.

"Place a bet," says he.

"A bet!" I am disgusted—almost.

"Go along now," he says, and I can see that he means business. "But leave the head here."

I have almost forgotten that all this time I am holding the box. I shrug, put the box on the bed, help Agnes to her feet, and take her out. She is pretty shaky, poor kid.

In the hall, she says: "I can trust Johnny, can't I?"

"You can trust us both," I tell her. But I cannot figure out what Johnny is up to.

In our room, I fix two drinks and hand one to Agnes.

"I guess he's right," she says. "The main thing is to get the head to the ship." She threw down her drink like she needed it. "We can call the authorities about—about my father once that's done."

"Sure," I say, pouring her another drink. She is beginning to get back some color. I jaw with her for nearly twenty minutes, and I am beginning to worry about Johnny, when in he comes, carrying the box.

"Listen, Pug," he says, "we've got to be careful—"

I interrupt him with: "What have you been up to?"

"Calling us a cab," he says. "I got the cab stand to tap Sleeping Bill. He'll be waiting out front."

"All that time!" I say. "And why didn't you call from here?"

"I didn't want that house dick—or anyone else—to know that anyone from this room was going any place. Now stop asking questions," he says, "and keep sharp." He looks at his watch. "We better get a move on, if we plan to make that ship."

What makes me edgy as we step out of the elevator is that the lobby is deserted. The yokel night clerk and his kid brother are nowhere in sight. But, as we are halfway to the front door, the house dick appears from a room behind the desk.

"Checking out?" he says. "Trying to skip on your bill?"

"We'll be coming back," says Johnny.

"Then," says the dick, "let's have your keys."

Johnny checks his watch. "We haven't much time," he says. "We better pay him."

We go back to the desk. I, for one, feeling kind of sheepish.

"What's the tab?" says Johnny, pulling Doc Schmitt's hundred dollar bill from his pocket.

"Ten G-s," says the dick. "You boys owe Sam the Elephant ten G's."

"Can't stop now," says Johnny, turning us about.

"Oh, yes you can," says the dick, pulling a gat. "Now, if you two and your lady friend will just step back into the office for a minute . . ."

Behind the desk, the dick does a quick frisk on me and Johnny. I guess he thinks he is too much of a gent to touch Agnes. He puts his own pistola away and holds Doc Schmitt's Mauser, taken from Johnny, pointed at us.

He orders us into the office with a jerk of his gun hand.

Who should be waiting for us there but Tweedledum and Tweedledee, our bonebreaking friends from Miami, the bad eggs in plaid suits.

The night clerk and his kid brother are sitting on a small couch, looking meek and mild.

The dick is behind us, blocking the door.

Tweedledum says: "We was just on our way up to see youse. Tanks for coming down."

Tweedledee says: "Mr. Elefanti wants his ten G's, Belmont. I hope for your sake that you have scored well during your brief stay here at the Bon Chance."

Johnny says: "I have, indeed, boys. As a matter of fact, we were off just now to collect a large sum. How about giving me an hour?"

"You must be nuts," says Tweedledum.

"Let's break his arms," says Tweedledee.

"Let's break his knees," says Tweedledum. "Then he can still deal from up his sleeves and make Mr. Elefanti's money back, but he can't run, see?"

"Pug," says Johnny, "we haven't got time for this right now" and I know what he means.

I grab Agnes by the arm and slam back with the box, knocking the Mauser from the dick's hand, as Johnny is making two stabs with his umbrella to the soft round bellies in plaid.

We jam through the door. I lose my grip on Agnes, and she falls. I pull her up, and we beat it out of the hotel to Sleeping Bill's phony Yellow Cab. But Sleeping Bill is not ready for our getaway. He is—sleeping.

Johnny pulls him out of the driver's seat, stuffs the C-note into his pocket, and we leave him standing there. I think he is still asleep as Johnny steers us out through the flood like we are in a motor launch. We head for the river, downtown.

At corners we are making huge wakes of water, which blur the night lights outside so they seem to run crazily down the windshield and windows. But through the back windows I can see headlights that are staying with us.

It is just like this when a shot smacks through the back window between Agnes and me and goes out the front by Johnny's ear, and Sleeping Bill's old car kind of faces one of these steel pylons, that are holding up the West Side Highway. Johnny is a smooth driver and pumps coolly on the brake, coaxing it, but Sleeping Bill's car has made up its mind. At the last second Johnny finds some traction and pulls the wheel sharp. The car leaps, avoiding a head-on, and slams into the pylon sidewise, on my side, back by the gas tank. Then we hear a puff.

"We're on fire!" cries Johnny. "Get out! Out!"

Now the three of us are running in deep water over slippery cobblestones.

I hear Sleeping Bill's phony old cab blow apart. Well, Johnny gave him a C-note, and the car was worth maybe only fifty bucks.

Up ahead of us is coming a police car, siren squawking. The cops in the car don't see us in the rain and the dark. They pass right by us.

I look over my shoulder and see that the Elephant's boys have negotiated a U-turn and are now heading off from whence they came.

Agnes says: "There's the ship! Follow me!"

Aboard, Agnes takes charge. "This way," she says, leading us through passageways. "Cabin A," she says. When we are at Cabin A, she opens the door and walks in ahead of us. We follow her into a good-sized stateroom, I guess you call it.

She crosses the room and turns around to us. Now she is not like Agnes at all. She is like some altogether different person. It is all in the look on her face. I get a cold chill up my back.

"Good morning, gentlemen," comes a voice from behind us.

I turn around and there are Von Heller and Lensky. He is holding his pistola with the silencer.

I am certainly confused. I look at Agnes. She is holding her daddy's Mauser.

"I'll take the package," says Agnes.

"What is going on here?" I say. I must admit I am by now feeling pretty stupid. I look at Johnny, and I am amazed to see that he is smiling. He sees that I am mentally in a bind and is good enough to answer my questions before I ask.

"We are rounding up secret agents, Pug," he says. "Uncle Wild Bill would be proud of us."

"What does he mean?" says Lensky to Agnes.

"I don't have the slightest idea," says Agnes.

"How did she come by the Mauser, Johnny?" I say.

“That falling act she did at the hotel. These two women—not to call them ladies—are aces at scooping up guns.”

“But Agnes,” I say, sadly depressed, “your father—”

“Doctor Schmitt wasn’t her father,” says Johnny.

The hatch now opens behind Von Heller and Lensky.

Two men with pistolas in their mitts step in.

“F.B.I.,” says one.

“C.I.A.” says the other.

“You might as well hand over your weapons,” says Johnny. “There’s a Coast Guard cutter blocking your way out to sea.”

The feds go around the room collecting from Von Heller, who has a nice little pearl-handled automatic of her own, and Lensky, and Agnes. When the F.B.I. agent is taking the Mauser from Agnes, Johnny says:

“Agnes, I’ve been meaning to tell you all night that you have beautiful legs. Would you mind lifting up your skirt so that I can get one good look at them before you go?”

Agnes gives Johnny a grim little smile, shrugs, and lifts her skirt. On her right thigh is a scabbard with a long knife in it.

“That’s what killed Schmitt,’ says Johnny. “Oh,” he adds, “thank you, Agnes. I shall never forget them.”

It is a week later and we are sitting in a couple of beach chairs by the pool of Sam the Elephant’s Miami Beach hotel. It is a glorious day and there are beautiful ladies stepping all around us and the noise of the diving board and splashing and palm fronds waving over our heads.

Sam the Elephant is in his gold bathing trunks and has a gold towel over one hairy shoulder and is wearing dark shades over his eyes and smoking a huge Havana cigar and sipping occasionally on a straw which draws up something green inside it. Johnny has been telling him the story, as follows, which clears things up for me too:

It seems that Agnes planned to slip away from Schmitt, with the head, at Penn Station, and catch the limo in which are waiting Von Heller and Lensky. The three were then going to drive to the freighter. The freighter was a Communist ship. Agnes, however, has been suspected of being a double agent. In Washington, she has been ordered to pose as Schmitt's daughter, but Schmitt has been warned not to trust her. Agnes, of course, does not know that Schmitt suspects her. Then Schmitt's inspiration about the Lost and Found, plus Johnny's bet with me, messes up her plans.

Later, she dumps Schmitt the hard way, with a knife, when the house dick leaves her alone with him, calls some contact with the freighter, and explains what has happened. She leaves word for Von Heller and Lensky to meet her at the freighter, and that she has a couple of suckers who will help her make the pier without interference.

Then she comes back to our room to tell us the story of Haydn's head, to make enough time elapse before we discover the body so that we will think Von Heller and Lensky have killed Schmitt. Also because the story will help convince us that she is in danger and needs help.

We go and find Schmitt, with me, at least, thinking what she wants us to think, that Von Heller and Lensky have paid Schmitt a visit. But Johnny doesn't think so. What troubles him is that Schmitt is stabbed in the back. Why should Lensky need to use a knife when he keeps waving around a revolver with a silencer on it? And why in the back?

That's when he thinks of Agnes. He sends me off with her to our room, but he keeps the head with him. He's afraid she will use the shiv on me, take the head, and scram.

(When I asked him how come he knows for sure that she has a knife, he says: "It was a logical deduction, Pug, from the circumstances—besides, I felt it on her thigh when I put her in the chair." He guffaws. "What about me?" I say. "She wouldn't tackle you, Johnny, because you had the Mauser. But suppose she used that pig-sticker on me?" Johnny says: "Why would she? She wanted to keep us with her. Besides, I had the head." Then he laughs and says: "I just had to gamble that she wouldn't knife you, Pug old boy." I say: "Thanks a lot!")

Then Johnny puts in a call to uncle Wild Bill Belmont, in Washington (He says: "I took great pleasure in waking him up at three in the morning"), gets the dope on the situation, and sets the trap at the pier.

Sam the Elephant is delighted with the whole story. He is also delighted that he will get his ten G's when we get the reward, which is to be within a month, from what we are told. But it is our nerve, says Sam the Elephant, which delights him most, the way we have come down to Miami and walked right in on him with our tale. Also, he is a great patriot, he tells us, and appreciates what we have done for our country. He is going to stake us until our money comes, and we will have the best.

He is laughing as he heaves himself up and waddles off, laughing and shaking his head.

A waiter comes out and passes him, bringing a telephone. It is Wild Bill in Washington has something to say.

Johnny is all smiles at first, but then he frowns.

"Wait a minute," he says, "are you sure?"

But I have already heard a click.

Johnny hangs up, looks at me, and says:

"Pug, we've got a problem."

"What's that?" I say.

"The head was a fake. The real skull has been with the Society of Friends of Music in Vienna since Eighteen Ninety-Five. The authenticity of the skull in their possession has been proven beyond doubt."

"A fake," I say. "Does that mean we do not get any reward?"

"I'm afraid not," he says. "It seems that Schmitt knew he was carrying a fake. He was under orders to do everything he could to convince Agnes that it was the real thing, and she believed it. And so did we."

"But, Johnny," I say, "now we owe Sam the Elephant the ten G's again—"

"Plus," says Johnny, "five hundred expense money."

"Not to mention," I add to the list of our woes, "our hotel bill."

"We better get packing, Pug," says Johnny.

“So it looks like we are on the run again,” I say with a sigh.

I am not overly interested in history, as I have a tendency to think that it is all in the past; but, for what I guess are obvious reasons, I stay interested in the subject of Haydn and his head. I follow it in the newspapers.

They finally get his head and the rest of him together in Nineteen Fifty-four in Burgenland. In Nineteen Fifty-five there is such a thing as an Austrian State Treaty, which is signed by the Four Powers. So it seems that nobody takes over Haydn’s country, which joins the U.N. in the same year. All this is very interesting to me, because I feel like, in a little way, I am a part of it. Also, when I think of it now, it brings back the days when Johnny and me were always on the run. Being on the run was a lot of fun if you ran with Johnny Belmont.

PART V.

AN EXPERIMENT IN GOVERNANCE

For some very important, and top-secret, reasons of State, the people who decided policy desired a change in the thought processes of the people they ruled, so they brought back the rusty old rack and began to stretch anyone who could not change his or her mind fast enough to suit them. Members of the public entered the Ministry of Thought at their natural height and came out about two inches taller. At last, we have become competitive, cried one of the people who decided policy. We shall become the capital of fashion, for we have some of the tallest models available. The Eureka-like quality of this observation caused the people who decided policy at the Ministry of Thought to completely forget what the very important, and top-secret, reasons were that caused them to bring back the rusty old rack in the first place. It was our intention from the beginning, they said with one voice, to open an international modeling agency: and things looked very promising for the new democracy until the people began to shrink back to their natural height, shrinking cartilage pulled down by gravity, as it were, and the people at the Ministry of Fashion, which the Ministry of Thought was now called, searched everywhere for their original reasons for bringing back the rusty old rack, but found that their drawers and filing cabinets, originally stuffed with strategic schemes, were now stuffed with dress patterns, Butterick having infiltrated the Ministry, which had become little more than a rag-shop. Such are the pitfalls of governance.

THE DEVIL'S TAVERN

There are three kinds of lies:
lies, damned lies, and statistics.
—attributed by Mark Twain to Benjamin Disraeli

Sam Stock is a man of his time, a hyperproductive computer programmer employed by the New York branch of the International Ministry of Wellness as a data analyst, a stat man, a Super Cruncher. He finds correlatives—hamburgers and high blood pressure, gum soles and flat feet, life and death (one-hundred percent). Everyone is at-risk. Life correlates to danger. But cyberchondria abounds. Sam thinks he might be contributing to the general unease. His work as a technocrat may have contributed to the fears of the public—their fear of walking, of breathing, of whispering (aspiration produces deadly micro-globules of sputum). This winter in New York people are lining up at the mobile Wellness Stations to get bat flu shots. Three cases had been reported in Miramar. The queues, Sam has noticed, are extraordinarily attenuated. People don't want to get near to one another. But of course, the bat flu shots are mandated. Those who do not get them are considered public enemies and are sought and found and sent on to mental health clinics. Just the other day, Sam saw that a group of senior citizens who protested the ban on donuts was rounded up and sent to the Senior Mental Health Center for examination. Sam Stock thought that, yes, they should have their heads examined. After all, carbs can be deadly, and some of those donuts pack icing—vanilla, strawberry, and chocolate; veritable guns of destruction. But there was something troubling about declaring all those old people insane.

Sam tries to balance these thoughts as he maneuvers the lunch hour streets in search of a health food stand. It depresses him to think of the recent ban on mustard. He had to admit that mustard was the only thing that made much of the proffered food of the city palatable. But he himself was the first to find the correlation between mustard and misbehavior. It was bruited about that upscale gangs of rebellious youth in Brooklyn were now attacking public officials with gobs of grey poupon, and of course there was that incident in Atlanta where the mayor was assaulted with deep-fried hush-puppies after instituting a ban on them.

Sometimes Sam Stock thought that officialdom was going a bit too far. He understood the impulse, natural to people in power, to tell others who have no power what to do. But sometimes . . . ah, a stand full of Free-Toes—sugar-free, carb-free, fat-free, and food-free. And not even a dab of mustard to put on them! Sometimes Sam Stock thinks that life is becoming tasteless . . . munch, munch.

Twenty-twenty, the centennial of Prohibition, that was a big year for the Ministry of Wellness! The events of that year included a world-wide ban on smoking, the

Bacon Act, and, perhaps the greatest coup the Ministry had ever effected, the institution of the Department of Mental Wellness, which allowed the authorities to take action against people who refused to care for themselves, people who puffed, tippled, or consumed food that was found by the experts at the Ministry of Wellness to be unhealthy. These slackers were of course costing us all money under the Universal Wellness Program. They were to be considered insane and sent to an asylum until they mended their thought-processing ways. Sometimes Sam Stock thought the authorities took advantage of this law to declare insane anyone who in his or her life of quiet desperation heard the sound of a different and distant drummer. It was from the dark underbelly that rumblings could be heard. There was the mysterious case of the physicist who smoked, the notorious case of the tippling mayor, the amazing case of the cake-eating songstress—these stories were heard of and retold, novelized on-line by rebel writers—*Smokey, The Mad Scientist, The Red Nosed Mayor of Castorbridge,* and *God Bless America: The Dreadful Story of Cake Smith.* Sam Stock reads these cautionary tales and tries to learn from them; but sometimes he yearns for romantic adventure. The idea of sharing a chocolate-covered donut with a beauty on a tiger-skin rug set his heart racing. His Free-Toe melts like icing in his mouth at the thought.

How could Sam Stock fail to notice Lorelei Rhinestein? She had been about the office for some time. But Sam is always intent on his production of correlatives. He sees another one—reading and suicide—and begins to run it. But he is distracted. Lorelei Rhinestein has lovely violet eyes. She reminds him of a flapper of eld. She has just come in from getting her bat flu shot and is flushed with . . . anxiety? The Ministry of Wellness does not want to tell the public about the many deaths correlating to bat flu shots. Sam Stock puts down "bat flu shots and death." He runs it—ummm! He looks at Lorelei Rhinestein. The flush is leaving her face. Not only will she live, he thinks, she will triumph. How not, with such eyes?

In the days following, he gets her name and her *modus vivendi*. She brings her own lunch. Fried chicken from home, long since banned from restaurants. She eats surreptitiously, suspicious even of associates. An atmosphere of danger clings to her drumstick. Sam Stock suspects her of transfats. He could see her in some ancient noir film, the banned-for-smoking "Casablanca" perhaps, still extant in cyberspace. Sam Stock blushes to think of it. Yes, he thought, she's like Ingrid Bergman—mysterious, beautiful, hat down over her violet eyes. But of course Ms. Rhinestein wears no hat. Though not yet banned, hats—with the one exception of cycling helmets—had been deemed bad for the circulation. The more fashionable members of the ruling class wore them; but, Sam Stock noted, Authority says yes to itself and no to everyone else. He bet that in secret they even ate cake. They did as they pleased.

Sam Stock is increasingly restive, so when Lorelei Rhinestein asks him for a date—a date with a woman of danger—he decides to give adventure a chance and finds himself saying—

"Delighted. Where shall we go?" Men do not ask women for dates, nor do they decide where their time shall be spent; men cautiously wait to be invited, and even here could be entrapment. Can mystery and candor exist simultaneously in enchanting violet eyes? Fling it, he tells himself, I'm taking a chance on love!

Lorelei Rhinestein wants to go to New Jersey. She knows a place out beyond the Pine Barrens. She drives them. It's Saturday night at the Jersey Devil's Tavern. Where are we, he wants to know, what is this place? What does it remind him of, dark and forebody with the moon overhead? In the woods, isolated, oh, what did they call them, roadhouses, speakeasies? Something out of cyberspace on-line noir dramas. "I don't like the looks of this," he tells Lorelei. His hackles rise, tickled, but really he does like the looks of the place. The place is like Lorelei herself, mysterious, beautiful in the moonlight, dangerous.

"I've been watching you, Sam Stock," says Lorelei. "I've been watching you and thinking maybe you need a real outing. If I'm wrong I think I can trust you to keep this to yourself, but if I'm right about you... well, we may be able to share something exciting. You don't look like a scaredy-cat. The last boy I brought here—a personnel director for the Nursing Corps—he ran away like a rabbit and got lost in the Pine Barrens for two days. First time he had missed a day's work in his life. He threatened to report me to the Ministry of Wellness, but I threatened to tell them that *he* was the one who brought *me* here and he kept his mouth shut."

"I'm not afraid," Sam Stock blusters. He is afraid but for some obscure reason it embarrasses him. Contradictions abound in a nature taught from childhood to be afraid of everything and at the same time to swim with

Bubbles, the friendly shark. Sam Stock allows himself to be led into the Jersey Devil. People sit at candlelit tables, drinking adult beverages, smoking cigarettes and cigars, or dancing to the strains of "Smoke Gets in Your Eyes." Seated, Lorelei orders the house cocktails, two Jersey Devils, looks over the flickering candle at Sam, and, in a low voice, sings—

> "They asked me how I knew
> My true love was true
> Oh, I of course replied
> Something here inside
> Cannot be denied . . . "

Sam tries to ignore her alluring, husky, melodious voice.

"What kind of place is this?" he asks, looking through a haze of smoke, here and there set aglow by dim lights.

Lorelei observes how wide his innocent blue eyes are in the mesmerizing undulation of the candlelight. "Sam Stock," she says, "this is a den of iniquity, a speak-drink-and-smoke-easy, and I have lured you here in order to make a criminal of you." She is saying this in such a manner that it sends a thrill of fear up Sam's spine, but then she laughs, and says, "Don't be afraid, Sammy," and Sam is so tense that he laughs too—a nervous hack—as the aromatic Jersey Devils arrive in tall, red, steaming glasses.

Three Jersey Devils later Sam finds himself smoking. At first he coughs but then he gets the hang of it and begins to like it.

"Inhale," urges Lorelei, and sings—

> "Oh, so I smile and say
> When a lovely flame dies
> Smoke gets in your eyes . . ."

Six months later, at work, Sam is dying for a cigarette. After all, smokers are people who have one friend no worse than others, the sometimes of their pleasure and the ultimate difficulties, the big troubles, the being able to be quiet in the hurried world, the holding hands without a word, the sad truth of the matter as recognized by ashes, or ashes recognized, whatever is looking up from nothing, from the smoke-filled no-bottom of everything, the oh for just a moment, the please slow it down, the oh God I'm late, the don't forget, the oh forgotten, but smokers are people who have at least one friend. The relationship between smoking and disease is merely a correlative one, he tells himself and the greatest correlation of all is life and death (100%), but right now he needs a cigarette. Everyone who has a moment of contentment, he tells himself, dies; therefore, contentment kills.

Minutes after this moment of illumination, Sam is arrested by the dreaded Green (really olive drab) Shirts of the Ministry of Wellness for smoking in the men's room and taken away to the insane asylum for mental reprogramming. His psychiatric report confirms that he may ultimately prove to be a danger to the State. He has a definite proclivity toward disrespect of authority. Sam says, "Authority says yes to itself and no to everyone else! It says No!" Sam tells Doctor Forbrane, his counselor, to shove it.

"And all this rebellion started with a single cigarette," Doctor Forbrane tells his colleagues over cigars and port. "Good thing we wiped out marijuana," he continues, stabbing his Montecristo into space for emphasis, "or all of the little people would have become non-productive. But have no fear. I have implanted in his brain a continuously ticking taser in order to pacify him. He will represent no more challenge to Authority than a popinjay. He will, in fact, become a useful member of society. Wellness will be his way!"

One year later, Lorelei meets Sam upon his release. "Are you cured?" she asks as she drives him away from the asylum.

"I'm fine now, but they caught me just in time. Got a cigarette?"

"In the glove compartment," Lorelei says, hitting the gas, heading for the Jersey Devil's Tavern, which, despite all efforts of the Green Shirts of the Ministry of Wellness, exists forever just beyond the Pine Barrens.

www.ingramcontent.com/pod-product-compliance
Lightning Source LLC
Chambersburg PA
CBHW030825310726
48980CB00006B/634/J

* 9 7 8 0 6 9 2 9 0 5 2 5 8 *